THE ALLOWAY FILES
E.J. ROLLER

New Stein Publishing House | Brooklyn

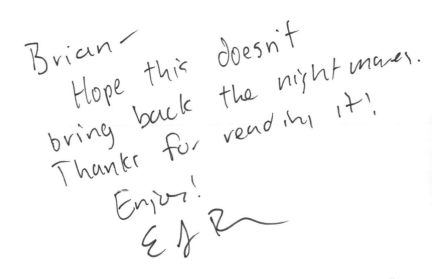

Brian—
Hope this doesn't
bring back the nightmares.
Thanks for reading it!
Enjoy!
E J R

2013 New Stein New Classic Paperback – First Edition

All rights reserved. Published simultaneously in the United States as an e-book and paperback by New Stein Publishing House, an independent publisher in Brooklyn, New York.

New Stein Publishing House
PO Box 380731
Brooklyn, NY 11238

ISBN: 978-1-940590-00-4

Cover Art by Betty Gipson
Book Design by Emily Roller
Headshot by William Roller

www.newsteinph.com

New Stein Publishing House is a small, independent publishing group—with an overflow of heart but a limited budget. If you like what you read, please help us by writing a review online, recommending it for a friend, or buying a copy for a loved one with similarly good

For the un-reformed.

THE ALLOWAY FILES

Prologue

Breyona Phillips wasn't the first person on the planet to feel sorry for Mr. Edward Winterblow. That much is certain. But she might very well have been the second.

Edward Winterblow was not an easy man to feel sorry for. He was the richest man on his block, and it was a nice block, too—the type with trees and a corner store that had organic products. Besides all that, he was lucky. He had a supportive wife, respectful children, cavity-free teeth, Google stock, and a '68 Ford Mustang. His only misfortune (which, until Breyona Phillips met him, was only considered a misfortune by Edward Winterblow himself) was a lack of misfortune.

But to Edward Winterblow, the lack of misfortune was misfortune indeed. When you have everything good in the world, all there is left to acquire is the bad. Edward Winterblow wanted the bad, needed the bad. It got to the point where, one unseasonably pleasant afternoon, he decided that he would seek it out. He would struggle; he would feel pain. He would, at least, feel *something*.

Before leaving his house, Edward Winterblow told his wife what he planned to do.

"That's a fantastic idea," she said. "Where will you go to find it?"

"I was thinking a public school."

"Oh, how perfect. You could substitute teach! There probably isn't a thing in the world worse than substituting for a public school! And Great Aunt Carol works for the City School HR Department. I bet she could find you a placement this morning! I'll give her a call."

The call was made, and the position assigned. "You're all set, honey!" said his wife.

Edward Winterblow just sighed and turned to his kids. "Behave yourselves while I'm gone," he said. "And don't forget to do your chores."

"Oh, Father!" said his children, "We always behave. And the chores are already done."

Edward Winterblow sighed again and exited his front door. He passed by his '68 Ford Mustang. He would walk today. Or take the bus if he could figure out how. A light breeze blew at his back as he started down the sidewalk toward the inner-city. He made it only one hundred yards on foot before he saw the sign: *Bus Stop*. He was still several yards from the stop when a crowded bus zipped past him, paused for a moment to load a couple teenagers, and then pulled away again.

Edward Winterblow was excited. He now knew what it felt like to miss the bus. But the thought had barely made its way into his brain when another, empty bus pulled up and opened its doors. The driver smiled at Edward Winterblow.

"It's your lucky day!" he said. "You caught the

good bus."

"The good bus?"

"That's right!" said the driver. "I always try to follow close behind the bus ahead of me—but just out of sight. That way the first bus gets crowded and this one stays comfortable."

"Oh," said Edward Winterblow, as he fished through his wallet for small bills. He only had twenties. "How much for a ride downtown?"

"$1.60."

"Do you give change?"

"Nope! But it's your lucky day times two!" said the driver before Edward Winterblow had time to relish in the loss of $18.40. "The machine's broken. No charge today. Head on back!"

Edward Winterblow frowned and climbed aboard. The bus took off. It hit every green light and reached the school in record time. He even had time to get a cup of coffee at Don's Gas and Grocery across the street.

"Where you off to?" asked the station attendant. Edward Winterblow told him. "Oh, well, no charge for coffee for teachers!" said the attendant. "God bless you."

Edward Winterblow said thanks and took a sip of the coffee. It was exactly how he liked it.

Edward Winterblow walked into the school building and immediately found the front office. The almost retired secretary had just given up on a terrible book and was headed to the supply closet to get a new one.

"That was a terrible book!" said the almost retired secretary as Edward Winterblow walked in. She was glad to have someone to say it to. "Now, what can I do for you?" Edward Winterblow told her who he was, and the secretary who was, conveniently, already at her supply closet, retrieved the keys from a hook on the door and handed them to him. "Room 201 is down the hall and to the right. This key is for the classroom; this one is for the bathroom." Then the secretary had a rare moment of generosity and handed him the terrible book she'd been reading. "Here, you can have this, too. You'll need something to do. There was a surprise field trip today, so you won't actually have any of the yahoos in your classroom," she explained. "Lucky you!"

Edward Winterblow thanked her for the book and went to the classroom, which he found easily.

No students showed up. Edward Winterblow read the book. It was poetry, which wasn't something that he'd generally read, but this one had such wonderful descriptions of regret and loss that Edward Winterblow almost felt like he felt something. But then he realized that he was just starting to get hungry.

That realization was coupled with an even more welcome one: He had forgotten his lunch. But before the pangs set it, the principal made an announcement:

"ATTENTION, TEACHERS. PLEASE PARDON THE INTERRUPTION TO YOUR INSTRUCTIONAL DAY. THERE IS LEFTOVER PINEAPPLE AND PEPPERONI PIZZA IN THE CAFETERIA. LEFTOVER PINEAPPLE AND PEPPPERONI PIZZA. THANK YOU. AND HAVE A PLEASANT AND PRODUCTIVE INSTRUCTIONAL DAY."

Pepperoni and pineapple pizza was Edward Winterblow's favorite. He went to the lunchroom. There were three pieces left. Edward ate one. Then another teacher came in, and Edward offered to split the remaining two.

"Thanks!" said the teacher across the hall. "Hey, we're going to Benny's after school. Do you want to join? It's trivia day."

Edward Winterblow said he would, mostly because he wasn't much good at trivia.

Teacher Happy Hour at Benny's was typically a sad time. But the teachers were in a good mood that day due to the surprise field trip. They had finished all their grading. Also, the bartender had two-for-one shots of Bulleit. Edward Winterblow loved Bulleit, and had never seen the pricey bourbon as a special anywhere else.

Edward Winterblow didn't possess a large store of knowledge, trivial or otherwise, but the category happened to be classic cars, his only hobby. His team won, thanks to him.

"Cheers to Mr. Winterblow," they said. The bartender gave him a $100 gift certificate.

But Edward Winterblow had had too good a time to want to come back, so he gave the gift certificate to a man lurking outside the door. The man was quite moved to receive it. So moved that he let go of the switchblade that he had been holding in his pocket to shake Edward Winterblow's hand.

Edward Winterblow said it was no problem and began walking toward the bus stop. He wasn't paying much attention, though, to where he was going. He walked directly in front of the very same bus that had brought him to town—this time headed in the opposite direction. Luckily, the lurking man saw the bus coming and pushed Edward Winterblow out of the way, just in time. They landed together on a soft patch of grass, un-bruised.

"Only patch of grass left in the City!" said the man.

"Whoo boy! That was close!" called out the driver. "Good thing I just got these brakes changed!"

Edward Winterblow climbed aboard the bus.

Every seat on the bus was taken except for one, near the front, right next to Breyona Phillips. She smiled. Normally, sitting next to a ripened City high school student in the late afternoon was not a pleasant experience, olfactarily or otherwise. But on this particular afternoon, thanks to the surprise field trip, which was to an air-conditioned movie theater, Breyona Phillips still smelled of lilac shampoo. And she also happened to be one of the most sensitive students in the district.

"OMG! You almost got smacked!" Breyona Phillips said.

"Yes," said Edward Winterblow.

"You not paying attention. What's wrong with you?"

Edward Winterblow looked at Breyona Phillips, and he could tell by the way she looked him right back in the eyes that she actually cared about what was wrong with him, that she was actually going to listen to what he said. So he told her all about the misfortunes of fortune. About the free bus ride, and the amazing book and the pizza and the $100 gift certificate. And, even though Breyona Phillips came from a poor background and sometimes didn't have enough to eat and was always made fun of at school for being overly sensitive—despite all that—Breyona Phillips understood his problem perfectly.

Edward Winterblow finished his sad tale just before his stop. He looked at Breyona Phillips. Breyona Phillips looked right back at him and said, "I feel sorry for you, Mr. Winterblow." Then she punched him, hard, in the balls.

Edward Winterblow doubled over in pain. He could barely breathe. The rest of the bus stifled giggles. Breyona Phillips nodded one time. She had finally helped Edward Winterblow experience the fortune of misfortune.

And Edward Winterblow felt that he'd had enough.

1

_____

Ms. Alloway faked a pull of her unlit cigarette and stared across South Avenue at a sign for Kingz Lake Trout. The sign, with its yellow background and red lettering stood out against the dark gray of the four-lane road, the light gray of the sidewalks, the faded gray of the run-down row houses, the rumbling gray of the clouds above, and the ominous gray of the school headquarters behind her.

It might be poetic, Ms. Alloway thought, though she was too foggy-minded herself to make it so. She was a twenty-six-year-old blonde, but her brain had already gone as gray as her surroundings.

Ms. Alloway took another fake drag of her real cigarette. She had never actually smoked, but she always took advantage of the union-negotiated thrice-daily fifteen-minute smoke break for teachers on administrative leave. She exhaled slowly. When she'd first arrived at South Avenue, it had been cold enough that she could produce a satisfying puff of condensed air. Now, it was just an invisible stream of hot breath that was absorbed immediately into the suffocating atmosphere.

Still, it was better than the Temporary Reassignment Room, where she spent the other six hours and fifteen minutes of her day under the watchful eye of Room Supervisor Ms. Suzanne L'Blanc. It wasn't Ms. Alloway's first stint in the Room. This time around, she was maintaining sanity by re-reorganizing her documentation—combining her behavior log and student-work portfolio into a single five-inch binder. She was hoping to find a sliver of meaning in this physical record of her dealings with individual students, meaning she could not discern in her intangible days with the group as a whole. It had been slow going, but after weeks of organizing, cutting, pasting, and rubber-cementing, she was nearly finished with the project. All that remained were scraps from one last student and some miscellany that she hadn't yet found a place for. Once that was completed, she'd either have her answers or would just have to find a new way to pass the time.

"Got a light?" said a voice immediately to her right.

Ms. Alloway frowned. She didn't like to have her smoke break interrupted, especially by disembodied voices. She turned slowly and inspected the John Doe who produced it. He had no distinguishing features whatsoever; he could have easily passed as a dark-skinned white, a light-skinned black, Hispanic, Native American, Asian or any mix thereof. He was likely somewhere between eighteen and forty years old; he stood about five-foot-ten; he wore mostly black; and he had short, dark hair. Ms. Alloway turned back to Kingz Lake Trout and immediately forgot what he looked like.

"Excuse me," John Doe repeated. "Got a light?"

"No," said Ms. Alloway. She waved the unlit cigarette toward him as proof.

"Oh, do *you* need a light?" said John Doe, produc-
ing a lighter from his pocket.

"No," said Ms. Alloway. "I don't smoke."

John Doe slipped a lighter from his pocket, lit his
own cigarette and stood for a moment contemplating
matters. "Trying to stop?" he asked, before taking a
long, sophisticated pull from his cigarette—a pull long
and sophisticated enough to produce a cough.

"Why'd you ask?" asked Ms. Alloway.

"Just to be friendly," said John Doe. "And supportive of your efforts to quit."

"No, why'd you ask for a light if you already had a
light?"

"Oh!" said John Doe. "Just to be friendly." Then,
after a pause: "I'm trying to start."

Ms. Alloway didn't care. She focused all her men-
tal energy on making John Doe stop talking, but he
continued.

"You like lake trout?" he asked, gesturing toward
the Kingz sign.

Ms. Alloway didn't reply.

"Theirs is pretty good," he said. "You might be
more of a grilled chicken kind of girl, though?

Ms. Alloway exhaled hot, invisible breath.

"Not a big talker, huh?"

Ms. Alloway shrugged. At this point, there was no
point to talking. Talking was as useless a form of
communication as screaming obscenities into a hurri-
cane. As waving in the pitch dark. As—

"That's probably for the best," said John Doe.

Ms. Alloway said nothing, annoyed that John Doe
interrupted her brief moment of poetic lucidity.

"I'm sorry," said John Doe, "I've been rude. I haven't even introduced myself." John Doe introduced himself and Ms. Alloway immediately forgot his name. She didn't tell him her name. Instead, she fake-finished her real cigarette, threw it on the ground, stepped on it, and twisted—like real smokers do. Then she picked it up like real smokers *should* and tossed it into a metal trashcan that was screwed into the concrete sidewalk. She glanced at her watch. She was only fourteen minutes into her break, but, if she walked slowly up the concrete stairs to the school headquarters, she could stretch it into the full fifteen. She started toward the school building, looking at her feet to ensure strides of no more than sixteen inches.

"Ms. Alloway," said John Doe.

Ms. Alloway stopped. She didn't much care for some John Doe mysteriously knowing her name.

"Ms. Alloway, I know."

"Know?" said Ms. Alloway. "Know what?"

"Exactly! I know what's wrong, and I know how to fix it."

Ms. Alloway studied him. John Doe put his cigarette to his lips, drawing out the moment: inhaling and then choking for several seconds, long enough that Ms. Alloway was going to be late. She turned to go. Still hacking, John Doe tapped Ms. Alloway on the shoulder and forced a folded piece of paper into her hands.

Ms. Alloway unfolded the piece of paper while John Doe caught his breath.

CITY SCHOOLS FORM 2.1.4 B
ADMINISTRATIVE LEAVE

Administrator: _Francine Fehler_   School ID: _405_   .
Employee's Name: _Ellen Alloway_   Employee ID: _065201_   .

Reason for leave: Please select all that apply.

- ○ Gross Misconduct
- ○ Refusal to complete required duties
- ○ Endangerment to students
- ○ Allegations from third party (if selected, attach allegations separately using form 2.1.5A.)
- ○ Refusal to cooperate with administration (if selected, please describe below)

  _____

- ☑ Other (if selected, please describe below)

  Pending investigation

Employee Statement of Acknowledgement:
By signing the form, I acknowledge that I understand the reason for my leave and agree to the conditions of administrative leave as outlined in the employee agreement, which may include Room assignment, temporary re-assignment, or filing duty.

_____ Date:_____

Principal or Administrative Signature
By signing the form, I hereby release the stated employee to the authority of the City School Central Office and agree to the terms outlined in the employee agreement in conjunction with the terms decided upon by City School Central Office.

Francine Fehler   Date: _1/26_

For Office of Human Capital Use Only
Date of form completion:
Expected length of leave:
Reassignment Location (if applicable):

"I already have a copy of this," said Ms. Alloway.

The coughing fit ended, and John Doe made a production of clearing the phlegm from his throat. Then he snatched the paper from her hands and tucked it into his jacket's inner pocket. "I know. But this isn't a copy."

"So?"

"There's not time to explain now. Meet me at 5.05 at Kingz—unless you'd prefer something grilled."

"Why?"

"I don't know, maybe you're watching your weight."

"No, why should I go to Kingz?"

"Their lake trout is the real thing. No substitute for the real thing but the real thing."

"Look—"

"Ahem," said John Doe—actually saying the word 'ahem' and non-nonchalantly pointed his elbow toward Hank Edwards, the octogenarian security guard, who had poked his head out of the handicapped entrance, just to the side of the front steps.

"Break's over, Miss Lady. L'Blanc said to stop lollygagging."

Ms. Alloway took one last look at John Doe, who had once again doubled over in a coughing fit. Ms. Alloway walked toward Mr. Edwards, who pointed his nightstick at the handicapped sign. "I don't see a limp!" he said.

Ms. Alloway rolled her eyes but took the extra steps to the main entrance, pushing through the heavy revolving door.

2

L'Blanc presided over the Room just as she had her classroom—with an iron first, an iron will, and coffee breath. She had been a classroom teacher for four years and a department head for one. When her school closed down and re-opened with a new name and the same students, she was offered the choice of going back to the classroom as a *regular* teacher or *managing* the Room. She didn't hesitate in her answer. She planted her substantial rear behind the long metal desk at the head of the windowless Room, and that was where it had been for the past fourteen years. Only Creepy McGoo, who had never actually done anything wrong—but with his mustache and crooked teeth, always looked like he was about to—had been in the Room longer than she. L'Blanc had been trying to get rid of him for years, mostly by shuffling him off to other departments in the school headquarters to 'help with filing,' but the other departments always sent him right back.

L'Blanc frowned at Ms. Alloway as she walked in. "You're late. Typical."

Ms. Alloway signed in. "Sorry," she said.

"If you were really sorry, you'd stop being late," L'Blanc said. "If you were really sorry, you wouldn't be here to begin with! If you were really sorry, you'd—" L'Blanc searched for another one but just couldn't find it. "Suffice it to say, Ms. Alloway, that your next break shall be shortened two minutes and twenty-seven seconds."

Creepy McGoo tried to give her a sympathetic look, but it came out so chilling that Ms. Alloway actually shivered. She quickly crossed to the opposite side of the room—to the desk that she'd occupied for the past two weeks. It was the second best desk in the room. The very best desk was in the corner directly behind Coach Humphrey. Coach Humphrey was the imposing basketball coach who famously "confronted" a member of the visiting squad's crowd with a folded chair. L'Blanc couldn't see around his wide frame, so the lucky occupant, blind Ms. Buttonworth, was more or less left alone. Ms. Buttonworth, of course, didn't properly appreciate the isolation. Ms. Alloway frowned at Ms. Buttonworth, but of course Ms. Buttonworth didn't notice.

"Let's make that two minutes and thirty-six seconds shorter—seat-up to seat-down," said L'Blanc. Ms. Alloway rolled her eyes. "It's that type of behavior that keeps landing you in the place!" said L'Blanc.

And she might very well have been correct for all Ms. Alloway knew. This was, after all, her third trip to the Room. The regulars were starting to recognize her. Coach Humphrey, who possessed a typical coach's compulsion to bestow uncreative nicknames on every living being that crossed his path, had a nickname for her: Rubber Cementer. In fact, by this trip, he even had a nickname for her nickname.

"Getting ready to RC something RC?" Coach Humphrey asked.

"They won't let me have rubber cement on my person," complained the whiney drug-dealing elementary teacher who sat on the other side of Ms. Alloway, in the third best seat in the Room.

"That's 'cause you're a whiney drug-dealing elementary school teacher," said Coach Humphrey, disgustedly.

L'Blanc said they should all quit their yapping; and Coach Humphrey said they weren't children and there were no rules about talking in the room; and the drug-dealing elementary school teacher explained that rubber cement wasn't a controlled substance; and Creepy McGoo smacked his lips for no good reason; and the two new teachers that Ms. Alloway hadn't met yet checked their phones; and Ms. Buttonworth stared blindly at Coach Humphrey's neck.

"Typical!" L'Blanc said. "Put away your phones."

"We're allowed to use phones in here," pointed out Coach Humphrey; and the whiney drug-dealer agreed, which made Coach Humphrey humph; and Creepy McGoo examined his left thumbnail, which he always kept long; and the new teachers watched him look at this thumb and inched their desks away; and Ms. Buttonworth just sat there, in the best seat in the room, growing older and blinder.

"This is why you're all here!"

"You're here, too," said one of the new teachers, a sour-faced thirty-something. For a moment, the rest of the Room looked at the new teacher. As long as she wasn't a sour-faced child molester, Ms. Alloway decided that they could be friends.

L'Blanc turned red. "You're one to talk Ms." She checked her roster. "Ms. Friedman. I've heard all about you."

"I'm Ms. Friedman," said the other new teacher.

"Really? You don't look like an alleged pedophile," L'Blanc said.

Ms. Friedman said that was because she was *not* an alleged pedophile; and L'Blanc said she must be some other sort of rotten, good-for-nothing slacker, then— like everyone else in the room. Coach Humphrey took offense at L'Blanc's generalization and proclaimed that it was completely untrue. They were all victims of a broken system—with the exception of the drug-dealing elementary school teacher; and the drug-dealing elementary school teacher took exception to the exception; and the sour-faced teacher who wasn't Ms. Friedman told everyone that her union rep was going to get her out of this shithole; and Creepy McGoo filed his other fingernails; and Ms. Buttonworth drooled a little.

The inmates were interrupted by a knock at the door. All heads turned.

"Got another one for you," said Mr. Edwards, nodding toward a well-groomed red-faced man. "Looks like a fairy."

The fairy said, "Excuse me?"

And Coach Humphrey said, "It's Tinker Bell"; and the whiney drug-dealing elementary teacher laughed; and the sour-faced teacher said that wasn't funny; and Creepy McGoo stroked his mustache; and Ms. Friedman shivered; and Ms. Alloway sighed; and L'Blanc pointed out that there were no more desks in the Room; and Mr. Edwards shrugged; and Ms. Buttonworth still wouldn't just retire.

"Fine," said L'Blanc, "We'll make room. Creepy McGoo, go see if the Department of Achievement and Accountability lab needs help."

"My name's Larry Wilson," said Creepy McGoo, peering around the room for a sympathetic look.

But the only person to make eye contact was Coach Humphrey, who scowled and asked if Creepy McGoo had a problem with his nickname. Coach Humphrey had worked hard to think that one up.

Creepy McGoo certainly did, but he certainly wasn't about to say so. He just tucked his head and slipped out of the room.

Tinker Bell eyed Creepy McGoo's vacant seat suspiciously. "Do you have sanitizer?" he asked.

"That's the sort of behavior that lands you in a place like this!" said L'Blanc.

"Sprinkle some fairy dust on it, Tinker Bell," suggested Coach Humphrey; and the whiney drug-dealing elementary school teacher complained that they wouldn't let him have sanitizer on his person; and the sour-faced teacher said she couldn't take one more minute of this; and Ms. Friedman pointed out that she had no choice; and Tinker Bell wrinkled his nose; and Ms. Buttonworth kept breathing.

The second hand made three orbits. A chilling shadow appeared behind the tinted glass of the door to the Room. Creepy McGoo knocked. No one got up to open the door, so Creepy McGoo opened it himself and stood in the doorway, directly under the sign that said: *Attitude is a little thing that makes a BIG difference.* "Guess who's back?" he asked.

Everyone felt uncomfortable.

"They sent me back, but they said you could send the Wallflower Girl."

Everyone looked at the mousey girl in the front corner of the room. They'd all forgotten about her. When Wallflower Girl first came to the Room, she had had laryngitis. In fact, that's why she was sent to the Room in the first place. She had laryngitis so badly that she couldn't explain to her administrator that she had laryngitis. Her administrator mistook the laryngitis for 'an attitude.' A week after arriving at the Room, Wallflower Girl's laryngitis had cleared up. But by that time, she'd fallen into the role of Wallflower Girl. And she knew that the first thing that she said would get a lot of attention. She wanted it to be profound, meaningful. But it was hard to find any meaning at all in the Room.

Wallflower Girl looked up mutely.

"Go on, then," said L'Blanc.

She left and everyone forgot about her again. Tinker Bell took Wallflower Girl's desk. Creepy McGoo went back to his usual spot and started combing his hair with a cheap plastic comb.

"I can't take one more minute of this," said the sour-faced teacher.

And the whiney drug-dealing teacher said he couldn't either; and Coach Humphrey didn't want to agree with him but felt the same way; and L'Blanc said it was exactly what they deserved; and Ms. Alloway checked out of the conversation.

She opened her documentation binder and flipped all the way to the front, to the "About Me" section. The copy of the unsigned administrative leave request that John Doe had just shown her was there, as were her priors.

3

Ms. Alloway's first term of administrative leave began on her second day of teaching.

"Principal Fehler wants to see you in her office," Ms. Noreen, the principal's almost retired secretary, had informed her at lunch.

"The principal? About what?"

Ms. Noreen frowned. "That's why you go to the office, Ms. Alloway. To find out."

Ms. Alloway went to the principal's inner-office where she sat across the desk and watched Principal Fehler slowly finish something green, lumpy, and re-heated. When the last drop had been slurped down, Principal Fehler looked up.

"I assume you know why you're here," she said, reaching into her desk and retrieving *City Schools Form 2.1.4 A.*

"Actually, no," said Ms. Alloway.

Principal Fehler waited. Ms. Alloway tried not to stare at a giant orange mole on her chin.

"I mean, did I do something wrong?" Ms. Alloway asked.

Principal Fehler waited.

"Is it about the Word Wall? I just don't see the purpose of having a Word Wall in a high school classroom."

Principal Fehler snorted disgustedly and wrote, *Refused to comply with Word Wall district policy* on the form. "Typical," she said.

"I didn't think it was a big deal. It seemed sort of juvenile."

"You didn't think it was a big deal?"

"I can put one up if it's that important."

"It's too late for that," said Principal Fehler.

"Why?"

"*Why?*"

"Why?"

"I assume you know why."

"Actually, no," said Ms. Alloway.

Principal Fehler waited.

"Was there some sort of deadline?"

"Was there some sort of deadline?" Principal Fehler mimicked, passing Ms. Alloway the form. "Sign."

"Sign?" Ms. Alloway hesitated.

"Are you really going to make me repeat it, Ms. Alloway? It's getting old."

"What's getting old?"

"*What's* getting old?"

"What's—"

"Sign the form, Ms. Alloway. Is there something about basic directions that you fail to understand?"

Ms. Alloway hesitated. "I don't understand why it matters if I sign."

"*Why it matters?*"

"Why does it matter?"

Principal Fehler slapped her hand on the desk.

Ms. Alloway waited.

23

"It doesn't actually matter," said Principal Fehler. "I can do this without your signature."

"You can?"

"I can. It doesn't matter whether you sign it or not, so you might as well do it."

Principal Fehler waited.

Ms. Alloway hesitated.

"Sign!"

"Fine!" Ms. Alloway signed.

"Now," said Principal Fehler, "take this to South Avenue. I think you need a little time for self-reflection before you return to classroom duty."

"South Avenue?"

"Ms. Noreen will give you directions."

Principal Fehler forced the form into Ms. Alloway's hand and shooed her out of the principal's office, slamming her office door shut. Ms. Alloway stood, stunned, in front of the secretary's desk. She heard the click of the lock to Principal Fehler's inner-office.

"Go south," said Ms. Noreen, without looking up from the book she was reading, "until you hit South Avenue. Then go left until you reach the school headquarters. But first give Erica the form to copy. You'll want one for your files."

Erica Meddler, the student office helper, took the form and disappeared for a moment into the copy room behind Ms. Noreen's desk.

"Wait! Just wait!" said Ms. Alloway when Erica handed her both copies. "What's going on here?"

Ms. Noreen turned a page in her novel.

"Excuse me!" said Ms. Alloway. "Could someone please tell me what's going on?"

"You bein' put out," explained Erica.

"This is completely ridiculous! I didn't do anything wrong!" said Ms. Alloway. Silence. Ms. Noreen turned another page in her book. "Am I losing it, or is this whole school crazy?"

Before Ms. Noreen had a chance to not respond, Dr. Luney, the assistant principal, walked in.

"Good morning, one and all! What a wonderful 405 day!" He smiled at Ms. Noreen, who didn't look up. He smiled at Ms. Alloway, who frowned. He smiled at Erica, who explained that Ms. Alloway was being put out. He smiled.

"Oh," said Dr. Luney. "Well, that's too bad! But don't take it personally, of course."

"Why wouldn't I take it personally?"

"Principal Fehler does it every year!" he said, smiling.

"Does what?"

"Puts a teacher on administrative leave on the second day of school."

"She can do that?"

"Of course! She's the principal."

"But don't the teachers have to do something wrong?"

"All teachers do *something* wrong. She just has to report it." Dr. Luney gave Ms. Alloway a sharp punch on the arm. "You'll be fine, though, kiddo! You'll be back in a week, well-rested and raring to go!"

Ms. Alloway rubbed her bicep. "A week!"

"Give or take."

"Give or take *what*?"

Dr. Luney squeezed his hands together and pushed out his lower lip sympathetically. "I am sensing you might still be upset," he said.

"Of course I'm upset."

"Is there anything I can do to help?"

Ms. Alloway just looked at him. Dr. Luney's face broke back into a smile. "It's all in the attitude, you know? Take it as a compliment."

"A compliment?"

"Sure! Principal Fehler always picks out the prettiest or smartest or blondest or ugliest or dumbest or meanest or nicest or fattest or skinniest or oldest or youngest teacher to put out on the second day. That means she must have seen something superlative in you, too!"

Then he disappeared into his office.

"South then left," said Ms. Noreen. "Or is there something about basic directions that you fail to comprehend?"

4

"Whatcha RCing now, RC?" asked Coach Humphrey.

"Documentation," said Ms. Alloway, quickly turning to the back of her binder. At the top of the page, she wrote: *Williams, Jazmine.*

"Humph," said Coach Humphrey, who didn't much care for documentation.

"That's why you're in here!" said Ms. L'Blanc.

And the other teachers in the Room started up again. Like they always did. This third stint in the Room was remarkably similar to the first. And the first was similar to the second. And the second to the third, of course. The minutes and the forms and the hours and the faces and the days and the conversations and the weeks ran together. Her smoke-break interaction with John Doe would have assimilated straight into her amorphous experience had it not been for one exceptional phrase: he said he knew.

What he knew, Ms. Alloway didn't know. Or, perhaps, she did know what he knew but he didn't know she knew it. Still, since she didn't know for sure if she knew what he thought she didn't know, Ms. Alloway couldn't let it go.

She replayed their conversation in her head but couldn't decide if the man was help in the midst of hopelessness or was unhelpful in her new-found hopefulness. "Where did this guy come from, anyway," she wondered, helplessly.

In fact, John Doe was officially hired, due to a clerical error, during Ms. Alloway's third stint in the Room. The clerical error was actually John Doe's—as he was a temp, specifically hired by the City School Human Resources Department to confirm the background of all City School new hires. John Doe had had no previous qualifications for such a duty. He had no qualifications for any duty. In fact, he hadn't even completed the second half of the application on QuickStaffSolutions.com when he received notice stating that he'd been accepted for the position.

But having received the job, he was determined to do it properly. And so, when it came time to verify his own application, John Doe followed procedure. Upon thorough investigation, John Doe found that he had not completed his application because he didn't have a transcript, because he didn't go to college. Deeper self-examination revealed that this was likely because he rebelled from an overbearing mother. She had expected him to major in business and run the family organic grocery, even though John Doe hated organic peas.

Upon finding his findings, John Doe immediately turned himself in to Manager Manly, manager of the Human Resources Department.

"It appears that this application is incomplete," he said.

"Does it?" asked dignified-looking Manager Manly, as he stroked his dignified-looking chin.

"It does. And I've confirmed it. The hire is not qualified for the position, temporarily or otherwise."

Manager Manly tapped his fingers on his desk. "This, this is difficult. I haven't had this sort of thing come up before. Do we have a procedure for this one?"

"Yes," said John Doe.

"Yes, of course we do. Which procedure would you recommend?" Manager Manly asked the question as though it were a test.

"I think you'll have to take the necessary steps for termination of the employee," said John Doe.

"Yes, of course. The necessary steps will be taken."

John Doe looked at Manager Manly. Manager Manly raised his glasses and closed his eyes and rubbed his nose, hoping John Doe would go away. After a few moments, he peeked. John Doe was still there. He looked back at the paper, cleared his throat in a dignified-sounding manner, and looked up again. John Doe didn't take the hint. "Look, I'll deal with it as I have time. I've got a stack of these to get through, after all. You can't expect me to deal with them all at once." He put it in a full tray labeled *In.* "Now, don't you have a job to do?" Manager Manly asked.

"I don't know."

"Oh, now you want to get smart with me, is that it?"

"The application was mine, sir."

"Oh, of course! Take it back, then!" Manager Manly handed the application back to John Doe.

"You don't understand—"

"I don't understand? Who do you think you are?

Why, I ought to fire you on the spot for this."

"I agree," said John Doe sincerely.

Manager Manly frowned. He couldn't tell if John Doe was smarter than he looked or dumber than he appeared. "Well, as long as you agree, then."

"But—"

"What?"

"The application, sir."

"I thought you were going to deal with it," said Manager Manly.

"I already dealt with it."

"Well, then it's taken care of."

"I think you might want to take a closer look."

"Of course I want to take a closer look! What do you think I am, an idiot?" He took the applicant back, held it up to his face, squinted at it. "Yes, well." Manager Manly hesitated. "You know it's rather hard to concentrate with you hovering right there. Do you mind?"

"Not at all!" said John Doe, who turned so that his back was to Manager Manly.

Manager Manly looked at the three rubber stamps on his desk. He couldn't remember where he was in his rotation. Manager Manly had a strict policy with his paperwork: for every five items, he approved three, rejected one, and marked one incomplete before passing them off to Carol for processing. The procedure had earned him his reputation as fair but strict. He looked over the last four items that he had stamped, which were sitting in an *OUT* tray. An application for the HR front desk position was rejected; an application for re-certification was marked incomplete, and a requests for medical leave and a petition for reimbursement for a continuing education course had been approved.

"Right," said Manager Manly. "I've made my decision."

John Doe turned around. Manager Manly picked up the *APPROVED* stamp and pressed it firmly in the upper right hand corner.

"Approved?" asked John Doe. "What does that mean?"

"It's means it's approved."

"So what happens next?"

"Carol takes care of that part. She'll let you know if we need anything further. Now, get back to work."

John Doe hesitated just a moment longer. Manager Manly placed the **APPROVED** application in the *OUT* tray and picked up the next item in the *IN* tray and began sounding it out. "Mr. Glenn Howard. Request for Medical Leave."

John Doe said, "So this approval is permanent, then?"

"I'm strict, but fair," said Manager Manly.

John Doe thanked him and left. Manager Manly breathed a dignified sigh of relief. Then he stamped Mr. Howard's request *REJECTED* and went on break.

5

Mr. Glenn Howard immediately teared up when he found his rejected medical leave request on top of the daily announcement memo in his school mailbox. He'd been losing his composure a lot for the past couple of days—really anytime he felt any emotion at all. He cried when he was sad; he cried when he was happy; he cried when he laughed; he cried when he was angry; he cried when he felt hopeful; and he cried for the hopelessness of it all.

As the warm tears began to slide down his cheeks, Mr. Howard couldn't stop himself from asking aloud, "Why? Why?"

"Oh, great," said Monsieur Richard, the dickhead French teacher who was just entering the faculty room. "Why *what*? What are they doing to us this time?" He pulled the announcement memo from his own mailbox and summarized the contents aloud: "Tacos today? Gross. Tray Chambers' memorial service this evening. Ha. You can imagine the sort of thugs and gangbangers *that's* gonna draw. Oh, shit! I see what it is. Another goddamned faculty meeting tomorrow? For fuck's sake! For the love of goddamned, fucking, bastard Jesus!" Monsieur Richard said, before begging pardon for his "French," instructing Mr. Howard to man up, and storming out of the room.

Mr. Howard slumped into a chair in the corner of the faculty room that smelled of mildew and cigarettes. "Why?" he said again, sinking into what he believed was depressed reflection on his failed leave request but was actually repressed deflection of the real problem at hand. "Why did they reject my request?"

Mr. Howard thought that if he could just have a couple of days to process, he'd be just fine. Like everyone else in the school. Just fine. "What's wrong with me?" Mr. Howard asked. "Why can't I man up?"

But why he couldn't man up wasn't the question that needed to be answered. The question that needed to be answered was why everyone else *could*. Because the fact of the matter was that three days ago, Tray Chambers had been shot twice in the stomach, bleeding out in the littered alley behind Mr. W's Chinese Takeout.

Mr. Howard didn't actually know Tray Chambers. He'd heard his name before and must have seen him in the hallway, but he had never had him in class. He couldn't quite picture his face.

Tray had apparently run around with some of Mr. Howard's students. Mr. Howard knew this because Breyona Phillips had immediately raised her hand on the morning that Principal Fehler had announced: "TEACHERS, PLEASE PARDON THIS INTERRUPTION TO YOUR INSTRUCTIONAL DAY. DUE TO THE RECENT TRAGEDY, COUNSELORS WILL BE AVAILABLE IN THE LIBRARY UNTIL LUNCH. STUDENTS, IF YOU WANT

TO SEE A COUNSELOR, PLEASE GET A PASS. PLEASE NOTE, ANY STUDENT WEARING A HOODIE WILL NOT BE ADMITTED. IT'S A SAFETY ISSUE! HAVE A PLEASANT AND PRODUCTIVE INSTRUCTIONAL DAY."

"M-m-mr. Howard, can I please get a p-p-pass?" she'd asked, sniffing loudly.

Mr. Howard replayed the rest of the scene from memory.

"Can I please get a p-p-pass?" Dontay mimicked.

"Oh, shit," Antonio said

"Antonio! Dontay! Please be sensitive to your classmates," Mr. Howard said.

"She frontin'," said Dontay.

Breyona sobbed. Mr. Howard wrote the pass and grabbed the roll of toilet paper sitting on his desk corner. A couple of candy wrappers fell out of the tube.

"You okay?" he asked.

"I told you, she okay. She just don't like your class. She didn't even know Tray-Tray," said Dontay.

"Tray and I had Fr-Fr-French," said Breyona.

"Well, then you'd know that he was never in Fr-Fr-French!"

"True," said Antonio. "He always running the halls last period."

"Every period!" corrected Dontay.

"True," said Antonio.

Mr. Howard moved between Breyona's and Dontay's desks. He handed Breyona the toilet paper and the pass and patted her shoulder. "Dontay, it's okay for Breyona to be sad about Tray. I'm sad about Tray. It was a tragedy. Everyone deals with—"

"Mr. Howard, no offense, but you not from here."

"People anywhere would be sad—"

"Mr. Howard," said Dontay, almost patiently. "She can't be sad 'bout someone she didn't know getting killed. Antonio knew Tray way better than Breyona, and he not actin' like a little pussy."

"True," said Antonio. "We live on the same block."

"I'm sorry to hear that, Antonio," said Mr. Howard. "Would you like a pass, too?"

"Nah, I lived on that block a long time," Antonio said.

"Since you hopped the fence!" said Gerald, who always had to say something.

"Shut the fuck up!" said Antonio.

"At least he makin' something of hisself!" said Janae, who had a crush on Gerald.

"Yeah, a dishwasher!"

"Better than a—"

"Antonio!" interrupted Mr. Howard. "You sure you don't want a pass?"

"Nah," said Antonio. Then, after a pause, "On second thought, yeah!" He winked at Dontay. "Could use me some peanut butter crackers."

"Least he not frontin'," said Dontay.

Mr. Howard walked Breyona and Antonio to the doorway. Dontay shouted after them, "She just wants attention. She didn't know Tray! Breyona, I can give you something real to cry about. You want something real to cry about?"

"Dontay!" Mr. Howard said. "Calm down!" Then to Breyona and Antonio, "Just go on. Don't worry about him."

Mr. Howard watched Breyona trudge down the hallway, sniffling; Antonio, who had practically skipped to the doorway, slowed once they were out of sight of the others in the classroom. He put his arm around Breyona. She leaned in. Mr. Howard went back inside his classroom. Dontay continued to yell. "You phony, Breyona! You phony!"

"Dontay!" said Mr. Howard. "I know you're sad, but don't take it out on Breyona. If you want a pass, I'll write you one."

"You don't know shit," said Dontay. "You ain't from here."

"I'm not from here, but at least where I'm from, we act like men. We don't pick on grieving girls."

Dontay stood suddenly. For a second, Mr. Howard was certain Dontay would hit him. The rest of the class thought so, too. Someone said, "Now you done it, Mr. Howard." Another said, "Dontay goin' beat your white ass."

But Dontay said, slowly, "I don't need no pass." Then he walked out, slamming the door behind him.

Mr. Howard watched him go. There was a moment of amused chatter among the remaining students while Mr. Howard still had his back to them. But as soon as he turned, and his students saw his face, they went completely quiet. Mr. Howard tried to tell them to resume their work, but he couldn't utter any coherent syllables. He went to his desk, and he wailed.

His students, kindly, had pretended not to notice. After all, he wasn't from there.

"Oh!" said Dr. Luney when he opened the door of the teacher's lounge to the sobbing Mr. Howard. "My goodness gracious sakes alive! What's eating at you?"

Mr. Howard waved the papers in his hand.

Dr. Luney grabbed the announcement paper and read through it: "Oh! Faculty meeting tomorrow. Those can be a bummer!" he said brightly. Then he squeezed Mr. Howard on the shoulder, leaving little marks where his fingernails cut in. "But don't let that get you down, Champ!"

Mr. Howard winced and sniffled.

"Get back up on the horse, Mister!"

Mr. Howard groaned.

Dr. Luney glanced at the door. "Well, come on now. Have some of this. It'll help you through." He offered him a blue water bottle.

Mr. Howard said he didn't need any water. Dr. Luney said it wasn't water.

6

Manager Manly returned from his break two hours later, ready to push through until lunch. He called John Doe back into his office.

"I think you might be able to guess what this is about."

John Doe thought so, too.

"It's become plain to me that our office is outdated," continued Manager Manly.

"Excuse me?"

"Our office," said Manager Manly, "is outdated." He waved his arms demonstratively, inviting John Doe to take in the office artifacts. "Did you know several other schools have transitioned from Human Resource Departments to Office of Human Capital? And here we are, living in the past."

"I see."

"Our procedures are ancient, too. Look at this *IN* tray."

John Doe looked at the *IN* tray.

"It's completely full of papers. This should be digitized."

"Digitized?"

"Yes, of course, digitized. And we need a website."

"We have a website."

Manager Manly paused. "Well, we need a digitized website."

"I think our website is digitized."

"Are you sure?"

"No."

"Well, could you check on that? I want it to be as digitized a website as humanly possible. And updated, too."

"What should be updated?"

"The name, of course. We can't keep calling ourselves a Department of Human Resources and expect to attract the best talent, can we? This is about jobs, son. From here on, we are the Office of Human Capital. Understand?" Manager Manly used his most serious hand gesture to convey the importance of the matter. "This is going to be your number one priority."

"But what about the background checks?"

"Son, this is about priorities."

"It is?"

"It is. And this is now your top priority. I need you to digitize!"

John Doe looked at Manager Manly. Manager Manly looked at John Doe. Manager Manly went through his entire repertoire of dignified gestures—the chin stroke, the nose rub, the lip purse, an eye widening, and finally an eye squinting. But John Doe just stood there. Finally, Manager Manly asked if John Doe could just send Carol in. He would be needing new stationery.

And so it was that John Doe began digitizing. His first top priority within his top priority was to scan in all newly-processed documents and drag them into a folder labeled *IN*. His other top priority within his top priority was to scan in the backlog of old files from the archives and drag them to another folder labeled *IN*.

John Doe, therefore, was scanning and dragging when City Teacher Union Representative Aliyah Deere arrived on the scene the next week. She arrived in style, accompanied by a herd of students. In addition to being the City Teacher Union Representative for School 405, Ms. Deere was the student council sponsor (SCS), the swimming coach (SC), and the black history club organizer (BHCO), which meant she always had the same seven involved students following her everywhere, like shadows. It also meant she didn't have time for bullshit. She swung open the office door so hard that she knocked over the maintenance man, who was scraping the letters *o-u-r-c-e* from the inside of the outer door. She apologized to the maintenance man by asking why they had letters on the inside of an office door, anyway, and then turned to John Doe.

"Don't bullshit me," City Teacher Union Representative Aliyah Deere, SCS, SC, BHCO, said. "I don't take kindly to bureaucracy. I'm City Teacher Union Representative Aliyah Deere, and I demand to know why Ellen Alloway is here this time."

John Doe looked up from the scanner and pointed to the children.

"What are they?"

"Students."

"Why are they here?"

"Job shadowing." City Teacher Union Representative Aliyah Deere, SCS, SC, BHCO, was also the job shadowing coordinator (JSC).

John Doe nodded and looked back at the computer to monitor its uploading progress. Something (though John Doe had no idea what, exactly) was causing the machinery to slow down significantly with each scan. The first few documents had taken just moments to upload. Now each was taking more than a minute.

"Excuse me!" said City Teacher Union Representative Aliyah Deere, SCS, SC, BHCO, JSC. "Young man, I need some information. Young man! I didn't come into this office to be ignored!" City Teacher Union Representative Aliyah Deere, SCS, SC, BHCO, JSC, banged on the counter with her fist, as did her seven shadows. "Sir! You! I can see you, you know."

John Doe looked up. "You're supposed to ring the bell if you require help," said John Doe, pointing to a sign on the front counter that said: *Ring the bell if you require help.*

"Why should I ring the bell when I can see you?"

"It's procedure. I don't work the front desk," explained John Doe. "It's not my priority."

City Teacher Union Representative Aliyah Deere, SCS, SC, BHCO, JSC, bopped the bell. John Doe continued scanning. City Teacher Union Representative Aliyah Deere, SCS, SC, BHCO, JSC, bopped the bell again. And again.

"What's all that racket about?" yelled Manager Manly from inside his office.

"Someone's at the front desk," John Doe yelled back.

"Don't we have a procedure for that?" said Manager Manly, as though it were a test.

"The procedure is to ring the bell for service," said John Doe.

"Right!" said Manager Manly.

City Teacher Union Representative, Aliyah Deere SCS, SC, BHCO, JSC, rang the bell again.

"Why is the bell still ringing?" asked Manager Manly.

"She still hasn't been serviced," said John Doe. "Should I make that my new number one priority?"

Manager Manly paused a moment to consider. "APPROVED!" he said.

John Doe walked slowly to the front counter and inquired as to the nature of her visit.

"Information! About Ellen Alloway. I came to find out why she was put on administrative leave."

"Could you please fill out this form?" John Doe asked, handing her *Form 2.8.1B, A Request for Employee Information.*

City Teacher Union Representative, Aliyah Deere SCS, SC, BHCO, JSC, frowned. She couldn't tell if John Doe were dumb as shit or just slow as shit. "I submitted this form last week."

"Is that right?" asked John Doe.

"Yes," said City Teacher Union Representative, Aliyah Deere SCS, SC, BHCO, JSC.

"Hmmm," said John Doe, holding it for precisely three m's. "Hmmmm," he repeated, holding it for four.

City Teacher Union Representative Aliyah Deere, SCS, SC, BHCO, JSC, pointed to a stack of forms in an *IN* tray on the front counter. "I think it's in there." Her shadows nodded.

John Doe went to the tray and started sifting through the papers, holding each one up for City Teacher Union Representative Aliyah Deere, SCS, SC, BHCO, JSC, to identify. Near the bottom of the stack, she said, "That one. That's it. See?"

John Doe examined the form. "This is *Form 2.8.1A*."

"Yes!" City Teacher Union Representative Aliyah Deere, SCS, SC, BHCO, JSC. "That's what you gave me last week."

"This one would go to the Human Resource Department."

"Yes!" said City Teacher Union Representative Aliyah Deere, SCS, SC, BHCO, JSC.

"The Human Resource Department no longer exists."

"What do you mean, it doesn't exist? Where am I standing?"

"This is the Office of Human Capital. We're starting fresh with a new system. I'll have to ask you to fill out another form." John Doe handed her *Form 2.8.1B*.

"This form is identical," said City Teacher Union Representative Aliyah Deere, SCS, SC, BHCO, JSC.

"It has a different letter at the end of the form title," explained John Doe. "For filing purposes."

"I'm not filling out another form. Where is your manager?"

John Doe pointed to Manager Manly's office.

"Could you please go get him?"

John Doe yelled for Manager Manly to come out. After a pause, he said, "APPROVED" and appeared with his dignified frown.

"What can I help you with?" Manager Manly asked.

"I need information on a teacher who was assigned to the Room," said City Teacher Union Representative Aliyah Deere, SCS, SC, BHCO, JSC.

"Did you complete the form?"

"Yes!"

John Doe whispered in Manager Manly's ear.

"I understand that you filled out an outdated form. Could I kindly ask that you fill out the relevant form?"

"I filled it out last week."

"We try to keep up with technology here," said Manager Manly. "It's about jobs. Modern ones."

"The forms are identical!"

"There's a different number," Manager Manly said. John Doe whispered in his ear again. "A different *letter*, I mean. For filing purposes. The new system has to know where to file the form."

"What if I just do this?" City Teacher Union Representative Aliyah Deere, SCS, SC, BHCO, JSC, pulled out a pen and turned the *A* into a sort of slanted *B*.

John Doe looked at Manager Manly. Manager Manly looked at City Teacher Union Representative Aliyah Deere, SCS, SC, BHCO, JSC. City Teacher Union Representative Aliyah Deere, SCS, SC, BHCO, JSC, looked from one to the other. The seven bored students gazed boredly at the ceiling. Manager Manly closed his eyes and counted to ten and rubbed the bridge of his nose. He opened his eyes. City Teacher Union Representative Aliyah Deere, SCS, SC, BHCO, JSC, was still there.

"Approved," said Manager Manly.

"That's called not taking bullshit," City Teacher Union Representative Aliyah Deere, SCS, SC, BHCO, JSC, explained to her students.

John Doe took the form from her and went to the *Aa – An* filing cabinet. "Look," he pointed out cheerfully, "It's the drawer I already had opened. I am only to the *Ak's* though. *Akers*, to be exact."

John Doe reached to the back of the file and yanked out Alloway, Ellen. "Big one!" he said. He opened the contents. "Now, let's see. You're looking for administrative leave *Form 2.1.4* . . . This one?" he handed City Teacher Union Representative Aliyah Deere, SCS, SC, BHCO, JSC, a form.

City Teacher Union Representative Aliyah Deere, SCS, SC, BHCO, JSC, read the form aloud, "*Administrative Leave for Ellen Alloway. Requested by Francine Fehler. Reason: Attempted Sabotage.* No, this is an old one."

"This one?" he handed her another.

"*Reason: Refused to comply with district Word Wall policy.* No, this is an even older one."

"Those are the only administrative leave forms. I can, however, verify that she has submitted all the proper documentation to the State for renewing her standard teaching certification."

"I don't care about that."

"You should. It's a State requirement."

"I just need her most recent referral for administrative leave."

John Doe looked at Manager Manly. Manager Manly looked at City Teacher Union Representative Aliyah Deere, SCS, SC, BHCO, JSC. City Teacher Union Representative Aliyah Deere, SCS, SC, BHCO, JSC, looked at her shadows and modeled eye rolling.

"It's not here," said John Doe.

"Carol!" shouted Manager Manly. "Carol, get out here."

Carol tottered out of the back office and smiled like a benign grandmother at the little congregation in the front office.

"Carol, have you seen a form for a Ms.—"

"Alloway. Ellen," said City Teacher Union Representative Aliyah Deere, SCS, SC, BHCO, JSC.

"Alloway, Ellen," said John Doe.

Carol tottered back into the office. Ninety-two seconds later, she emerged with a form for John Doe and eight Werther's Originals for the visitors. "This what you need?"

She handed the form to John Doe. John Doe handed the form to Manager Manly. Manager Manly handed City Teacher Union Representative Aliyah Deere, SCS, SC, BHCO, JSC, the form.

City Teacher Union Representative Aliyah Deere, SCS, SC, BHCO, JSC, said, "It says, *Pending Investigation* as the reason. What does that mean?"

John Doe looked at Manager Manly. Manager Manly stroked his chin. Then he cleared his throat. Then he said, "It means it's still under investigation."

"For what?" asked City Teacher Union Representative Aliyah Deere, SCS, SC, BHCO, JSC.

"That's what we're investigating."

"Who's investigating?"

She looked at Manager Manly. Manager Manly looked at John Doe. John Doe would have looked at Carol, but she had just shut the door to the back office.

"He is," said Manager Manly, pointing to John Doe.

"Well?" said City Teacher Union Representative Aliyah Deere, SCS, SC, BHCO, JSC.

"Well?" echoed her shadows.

7

John Doe began his investigation the next morning at the main office of School 405. The almost retired secretary, Ms. Noreen, ignored John Doe until a bead of sweat dripped from her forehead onto the book she was reading. "You're letting the air out," she finally said without looking up.

"Excuse me?"

"The air conditioning. You're standing in the doorway and letting the air escape. It's getting hot." If she had wanted to drip sweat all day, Ms. Noreen would have been a teacher.

"Oh, sorry."

John Doe stepped in and closed the door. Ms. Noreen kept reading. She was getting to the good part. John Doe cleared his throat. Twice. Ms. Noreen rolled her eyes and said, "If you have something to say, say it."

"I'm from South Avenue," he said.

Ms. Noreen glanced up. "Why didn't you say so?" she said. "The classroom should be ready to go. Should be a stack of worksheets on the desk. She stood and went to her office closet and pulled out two keys.

"This one is for the bathroom; this one is for the class-room."

"Excuse me?"

Ms. Noreen repeated slower, "This one," she held up a key, "Is for the bathroom. This one," she held up the other key, "Is for the classroom where you will be substituting. Bathroom," she raised the first key. "Classroom," she raised the second.

"I think there has been some misunderstanding," said John Doe.

"Oh, boy, South Avenue is really scraping the bottom of the barrel for substitutes, huh? Look, just try each one until you get it right, okay."

"I don't think I need keys."

"You do if you want to use the restroom. We keep them locked all day. Too many bathroom fires. Now they have to be supervised at all times. If your students want to use the restroom, you can write them a pass to the office, and they can wait right here until I'm available to let them in." Ms. Noreen nodded to a group of frowning students behind him, who were shifting their weight from one foot to the other.

"Mister, will you let us in now?" one of them asked.

"He can't let you in! He has a class to teach," answered Ms. Noreen. "You should have gone at home!" she added. "It's not like these yahoos don't know the policy," she said to John Doe. Then she turned to the students. "It's not like you yahoos don't know the policy."

"It's a fucking stupid policy," said one student.

"Yeah? Well, that's going to be another ten minutes, now." Ms. Noreen liked putting tasks off for ten minutes; it meant she'd be ten minutes closer to retirement when she finished them.

"Shut the fuck up, T.J.! You know how she be."

Ms. Noreen shook her head for John Doe's bene-fit. "How she be? Do you hear that? And they wonder why these kids fail English."

Another student entered the office.

"Good God!" said Ms. Noreen. "You all guzzling iced tea on the bus or something?"

The student held out a sheet of paper. "Ms. Eagle-ton asked if she could have twenty copies of this."

Ms. Noreen took the paper without saying any-thing. The student lingered.

"OK," said Ms. Noreen. "You gave me the paper. Go on back to class."

"Ms. Eagleton said to wait for the copies. We need them in class now."

"Oh, did she?" Ms. Noreen rolled her eyes at John Doe. "Well, tell Ms. Eagleton that if she didn't wait until the last minute to make her lesson plans that she might be able to get her copies on time. Some of us are busy. Look at this office! Lack of preparation on her part doesn't constitute an emergency on mine, does it now?" Ms. Noreen asked, repeating the slogan that she had on a poster on the front of her desk as well as on her coffee mug.

The student remained in the office.

"Good God," said Ms. Noreen. "Well, go wait with the others, then. I'll get to you after I take these yahoos to the bathroom."

The student shrugged and said the air condition-ing in the main office felt good anyway. It was already 88 degrees in Ms. Eagleton's classroom.

"See how much they whine?" Ms. Noreen said to John Doe. Then she turned to the kids. "You all whine too much!"

T.J. said, "Just let us go to the bathroom."

"That's another ten!" she said.

"Dammit, T.J.!" said another student.

Ms. Noreen turned back to John Doe. "See what I have to put up with? It's like this all the time. ALL THE TIME. They don't pay me enough to deal with these yahoos. Now where were we?" Ms. Noreen sat back down at her desk. "Oh, right. You'll be in room 201, up the stairs and down the hall to the right."

"I'm not—"

"You're not what!" asked Ms. Noreen in such a frightening tone that John Doe forgot what he wasn't. Ms. Noreen continued. "I swear to God, I'm just counting the minutes to retirement. How much can a woman take? You know how much they pay me?" Ms. Noreen paused to give John Doe time to consider and answer the question. When he didn't, she said, "Well, it's none of your damn business how much they pay me, anyway."

Ms. Noreen picked up her book and found her place.

"Just ask if you get lost. Everything you need should be on the desk. If you have an emergency, you'll have to stick your head out in the hallway and holler, because I don't have time to explain to you how the intercom works. Maybe the kids will. Do you have any questions now?" Ms. Noreen didn't pause. "Good, because you're already minutes late for first period." She nodded to the door. "Let us know if you have any questions. Or ask a student. Seems the yahoos run the place these days anyway."

John Doe left the office.

"Shut the door!" yelled Ms. Noreen. "It's already

88 degrees out there!"

8

John Doe found the staircase and made his way to a classroom with a sign that said *Room 201. Ms. Alloway, English III.* John Doe entered the room. Four students sat among the twenty-eight desks: a girl holding a book; another holding a phone; a third powdering her nose; and a boy who was passed out on his desk and drooling into a slowly expanding puddle.

"Is this room 201?" asked John Doe.

The one with the phone rolled her eyes. The one with the makeup powdered. The sleeping one drooled. The one with the book nodded.

"Are you our new substitute?" the one with the book asked.

"Yes," said John Doe. "I guess so."

The one with the book looked at John Doe. The others carried on with their prior activities. John Doe looked at the teacher's desk. There were a few papers there. He picked up the one titled *First Period Roster.* There were thirty-six students on the roster.

"Guess I should call attendance," said John Doe.

The one with the book nodded. The one with the phone snorted.

John Doe said, "Destiny Adler." The one with the phone said, "Here." The one with the book frowned and just barely shook her head. John Doe wrote *Present* next to Destiny's name.

"Robert Anderson."

"Here," said the one with the phone without looking up from her electronic device.

"But you were Destiny," said John Doe.

"I'm Robert, too," said the one with the phone.

The one with the book shook her head.

"You don't look like a Robert."

"You don't look like a sub," said the one putting on makeup.

"She not Robert," said the one with the book.

"Don't you be snitching," said the one with the phone to her. The one with the book looked back at her book.

John Doe continued, "Imani Baker."

"It's pronounced like with an *ee* sound," corrected the one with the phone.

"*Ee*—" began John Doe, but he was interrupted by an important announcement from the beige speaker on the wall directly above the teacher's desk.

"PLEASE EXCUSE THIS INTERUPTION TO YOUR INSTRUCTIONAL DAY! IT HAS COME TO MY ATTENTION THAT SOME TEACHERS HAVE PERSONAL COFFEE MAKERS IN THEIR CLASSROOMS. THIS IS NOT ALLOWED. IT'S A SAFETY ISSUE! PLEASE REMOVE THESE DANGEROUS FIRE HAZARDS FROM YOUR ROOM IMMEDIATELY. I REPEAT, COFFEE MAKERS ARE A SAFETY ISSUE. THANK YOU. PLEASE HAVE A PLEASANT AND PRODUCTIVE INSTRUCTIONAL DAY."

John Doe blinked for a moment, trying to remember where he was.

"*Ee-man,*" the one with the book, helped.

"*Ee-man-eye,*" said John Doe.

"*Ee-man-ee,*" corrected the one with the phone.

"*Ee-man-ee,*" said John Doe.

"Here," said the one with the phone.

"Of course," said John Doe. "I suppose you're Tray Chambers, too."

"No, he dead."

The one with the book looked down. Her lips quivered. The one with the makeup looked into her handheld mirror—and then switched from powder to eyeliner.

"Look," said John Doe. "I know I'm just a substitute, but—"

"Where's Ms. Alloway?" said the one with the phone.

"But if you would just *tell* me your names—"

"What's it to you?" said the one with the phone.

"I'm Breyona Phillips," said the one with the book. She pointed to the one with the makeup. "That's Erica. And that's Antonio sleeping over there," she said, pointing to the drooling boy. "He work late," she explained. "And—"

"Don't you dare!" said the one with the phone.

"Come on," said John Doe. "Don't you want to be marked present?"

"They'll mark us present anyway. No one collects that," said Erica. "I'm an office worker," she explained. "I know things."

Breyona shrugged. John Doe set the roster back down on the desk. He looked at his watch and compared it to the classroom clock that was in the upper left hand corner between a laminated flag and poster that said, *Be the Change You Want To See In The World.* The clock was a little fast. Or maybe his watch was slow.

"So," said John Doe. "What have you all been working on?"

"Preparing for the State Exams," said Breyona. "There should be new worksheets on your desk."

John Doe found the large pile of worksheets and handed one each to Erica and Breyona and slid another under Antonio's folded arm. When he got to the girl with the phone, he bent at the waist, trying to keep as much physical distance as possible, and set the paper on the corner of her desk. But it swooped to the floor. John Doe hesitated a moment, unsure if he should move further into her space to pick it up. He was saved the decision by an announcement from Erica: "DONE!" she said. "Check it! The answer sheet should be at the bottom of the pile."

"But you didn't even have time to read the passage."

"It's test prep!" said Erica, "You not supposed to read it. We have test-taking skills."

John Doe checked it. Erica had chosen *C* on every question. She got six out of ten correct. Breyona took several minutes to read her questions through. Then she used process of elimination to take away answers she knew were incorrect. Then she chose the best answer from the remaining choices—though she overthought several of them. She also got six out of ten correct.

John Doe told them both good job and asked if they were doing anything besides test prep.

"Nope," said the one with the phone.

"Well, with Ms. Alloway we were reading *To Kill a Mockingbird*," said Breyona, holding up the book she had been reading.

"It's a dumb book," said the one with the phone.

"You liked it when Ms. Alloway read it," said Breyona.

"It's a dumb book," said the one with the phone.

"Jazmine liked it when Ms. Alloway read it," said Breyona, this time addressing John Doe.

"Now you be calling out my name," said Jazmine.

"Chill," said Breyona.

"*Chill?*"

"JK. It was an accident."

For a moment it looked as though Jazmine might get out of her seat. Instead, she resumed typing on her phone. "You were an accident."

Antonio snorted in his sleep.

"Should we keep reading?" asked John Doe.

"Yes!" said Breyona.

"Whatever," said Jazmine.

Erica picked at a pimple.

Breyona told him the page they were on. John Doe looked around for another copy of the book. He looked in the teacher's desk, under the teacher's desk, under the student desks, on the bookshelves, which were empty aside from some workbooks titled *TESTING SUCCESS*. Breyona watched. Erica powdered. Jazmine poked at her phone. Antonio slept.

"Do you know where there might be another copy?" John Doe finally asked.

"Up yo' ass," said Jazmine. Breyona shook her head. Antonio coughed.

"Mrs. Brown has them," said Erica.

"Who's Mrs. Brown?"

"The librarian. She doesn't allow books in unattended classrooms."

"I'm attending the classroom," said John Doe.

"Right," said Erica shaking her head. She paused. "1 can go ask her for another copy. Write me a pass?"

John Doe wrote her a pass.

Erica closed her mirror, tossed her makeup into her purse, pulled her purse straps over her shoulder, and flashed a peace sign. "Deuces!" she said. Then she trotted out the door. Ten seconds of silence passed.

"You know she not coming back, right?" said Jazmine.

"I'll go!" said Breyona, gathering her things. "Write me a pass?"

9

Mrs. Brown had a responsibility, a major one. She was guardian of the most precious resource the world had ever had, knowledge. And she was not about to let it escape her sight. Before she was hired for School 405, 29.8% of the school's books went unreturned each year. Since she'd arrived, only 14.2% had gone missing. Statistically significant improvements like that only happened with dedication, vigilance, and strict check-out procedures. So she wasn't about to let down her guard for little Breyona Phillips, no matter how politely the little hooligan might ask. Chances were too high that if she let Breyona take a book from the library, it wouldn't be coming back.

"What do you mean you need another copy of *To Kill a Mockingbird*?" she asked, keeping the tone light but eyeing the young girl suspiciously.

"The sub asked for one."

"A sub? What on earth would a sub do with a book?"

"He said he was going to read it."

"He was going to read it? You mean, to himself?"

"No, aloud. It was what we were reading before

he came."

Mrs. Brown was not about to buy that one. A sub wouldn't read a book aloud to a class. Mrs. Brown looked at Breyona. Breyona looked at Mrs. Brown.

"You really think that man was planning on reading the book aloud to you?"

Breyona nodded. "Please?" she tried.

"You understand, don't you, that I have a responsibility."

Breyona nodded.

"A big one."

Breyona nodded.

"We can't just let our books leave this place all willy-nilly can we?"

Breyona shook her head. Mrs. Brown patted it. "I thought you'd understand. Run along back to class, then."

"But can't you just let us borrow—"

"Sweetie, what does this place look like?" Breyona and Mrs. Brown looked at the mostly full bookshelves that lined the walls of the library, which surrounded several round, empty tables. "You think this is a Block Buster or something?"

"What's a Block Buster?" asked Breyona.

Mrs. Brown tried a different tact, still keeping her tone sweet. "What do you think would happen if I let every kid in this school come in and borrow a book, huh? How much longer do you think we'd have books? You think books grow on trees?"

"No, ma'am," said Breyona.

"So why don't you just run along and tell your sub that he can find something else for you all to do today, OK? OK." Mrs. Brown started pulling the girl by the elbow toward the door.

"We just need two copies, though," said Breyona. Mrs. Brown stopped. She had never seen such a persistent student. It was highly suspect.

"Why do you want these books so badly?"

"To read."

"To read?"

"Just to read."

"Just to read? Where do you think novels are going to get you, huh?"

"But—"

"And this book is well above the average reading level for students in this school. Have you seen the test scores?"

"No."

"Well, I have. And I know this book is much too hard. If you try to read this one, you will just get discouraged and quit. That would be terrible for your morale."

"It would?"

"Of course it would. How silly do you think you'll feel when you get to a word or phrase that you don't know?"

"IDK," she said.

"What?"

"What *what*?"

"What did you just say?"

"I don't know."

"Oh, forget it then," said Mrs. Brown. "Just take it from me. You're not ready for this book."

"But Ms. Alloway—"

"Oh, I see. You have an English teacher who has told you that books are important."

"Yes—"

"She's teaching you *books* instead of teaching you

skills, huh?"

"She was just reading it—"

"Let me ask you something: Will you EVER need to know the plot to *To Kill a Mockingbird* to get a skilled job?"

"I don't know," Breyona hesitated. "No?"

"Will you ever need to be able to finish an entire novel to get a skilled job?"

"I don't know."

"Let's put it this way: how many jobs out there allow you to just sit around reading novels all day."

"You get to read."

"Well, of course, I read novels!" said Mrs. Brown. "I'm a librarian. I've read sixty-two books so far this year. Sixty-two! That's almost a book a day. But do you think *you're* going to be a librarian?"

"No ma'am."

"Are you going to teach English?"

"No."

"So, statistically speaking, you'll most likely never need to read anything more difficult than a manual. You need manual-reading skills. SKILLS!"

Mrs. Brown had worked herself into a sweat by now.

"Skills?"

"Skills! Not stories. Don't let those teachers try to turn you into English majors."

"Why?"

"English majors starve."

"Oh," said Breyona. Then she paused and reached into her handbag. "You should probably take this one, too, then." She produced her own copy of *To Kill a Mockingbird*. Mrs. Brown smiled and patted her head. "That's a good girl!" She helped her out the door and closed it behind her. Then she sat down, proudly, at her desk and pulled out her ledger. Her theft rate was now down to 13.9%. She was inarguably the best librarian the school had ever had. Statistics don't lie.

10

John Doe softly whistled a tune from *Hairspray*. Jazmine texted. Antonio slept. John Doe tossed his pen in the air and caught it. Jazmine texted. Antonio slept. John Doe tossed his pen in the air but dropped it. Jazmine texted. Antonio slept. John Doe couldn't take it any longer. He had to break the silence.

"So," he said to Jazmine. "Who are you texting?"

Before Jazmine had a chance to tell him to stop snooping in other people's business and find some other way to entertain his own damn self, Breyona came back. She set her purse back under her desk and folded her hands on her desk and looked up at John Doe.

"Did you get the book?"

"No," said Breyona.

"Well, I could just borrow yours."

"She took that one, too."

"She what?" said John Doe.

"She what?" mimicked Jazmine.

"She said we should work on skills."

"On skills?" said John Doe.

"On skills?" mimicked Jazmine. She lowered her

phone. "You have a charger, sub?"

"No."

"Damn," said Jazmine. "You a clown."

"A clown?" asked John Doe.

Jazmine set her dead phone on her desk and pulled out a black, permanent marker. She talked as she drew on her desk. "You wanna talk?" she asked. "Let's talk. When's Ms. Alloway coming back."

"I don't know."

"Why's she gone?"

"That's what I'm trying to figure out," said John Doe.

"What do you mean, you're trying to figure it out? I thought you just a sub."

"You could work with us on skills," suggested Breyona.

"Shut up," said Jazmine. "I'm talking to this man. I knew he was phony. Real subs don't try to teach."

"ATTENTION STUDENTS AND TEACHERS! PLEASE PARDON THIS INTERRUPTION TO YOUR INSTRUCTIONAL DAY! WE HAVE HAD A CHANGE IN THE LUNCH MENU THIS AFTERNOON. WE WILL BE HAVING TACOS. I REPEAT, THERE IS A CHANGE IN THE LUNCH MENU THIS AFTERNOON. WE WILL BE HAVING TACOS. NOT PIZZA. TACOS. THANK YOU FOR YOUR ATTENTION. PLEASE PROCEED WITH YOUR REGULAR INSTRUCTIONAL DAY."

"I like tacos!" said Breyona.

"Shut the fuck up, Breyona," said Jazmine.

"We had them yesterday, too," said Breyona. "But I think they be better on the second day."

"I swear to God if we weren't cousins, I'd tear

your cheap-ass weave right off your head." Jazmine turned to John Doe. "What were we talking about?"

"Skills," said Breyona. "What skills do you have?"

"Subs don't have skills. Why you think they're subs?"

"Actually—"

"TEACHERS AND STUDENTS! PLEASE PARDON THIS SECOND INTERRUPTION TO YOUR INSTRUCTIONAL DAY. I HAVE BEEN INFORMED THAT I WAS MISINFORMED ABOUT THE CHANGE IN LUNCH. WE ARE STILL HAVING PIZZA TODAY. I REPEAT. WE ARE STILL HAVING PIZZA TODAY. THANK YOU FOR YOUR ATTENTION. PLEASE HAVE A PLEASANT AND PRODUCTIVE REGULAR INSTRUCTIONAL DAY."

"Aw, man!" said Breyona.

"I don't know how you eat that dirty-ass food anyway."

"The tacos are pretty good."

"I WOULD ALSO LIKE TO REMIND YOU TEACHERS TO REMOVE COFFEE MAKERS AND ANY OTHER ELECTRONIC APPLIANCES THAT YOU MAY HAVE IN YOUR CLASS-ROOM. THIS IS A SAFETY ISSUE. PLEASE HAVE A PLEASANT AND PRODUCTIVE REGULAR INSTRUCTIONAL DAY.

Jazmine looked at Breyona then at the sub, trying to remember who it was that she meant to berate.

Antonio popped his head up. "Tres, dos, uno," he counted down. The bell rang. He got up and left.

"He always be doing that!" said Breyona, gathering her things and following him out the door. "Freaks me out."

Jazmine put her phone in her purse. "So, you a snitch?" she asked before leaving.

"I'm not snitching per se."

"Everyone always snitches on the good teachers. You gonna snitch, snitch on Monsieur Richard. He a dickhead."

11

Monsieur Richard was a dickhead. A 5'4" shiny-topped dickhead, to be exact. Though, like most dickheads, he preferred to label himself a *realist*. He taught French, and his teaching philosophy was: *These kids won't ever go to France, anyway.* And if you didn't like it, he'd just say, "Well, it's true, isn't it?"

He spent most of his classroom time forcing students to read French passages aloud and then mimicking their pronunciation.

"*Jay soos dicks-sept? Jay soos dicks-sept?* Nice try. Good luck getting into an R-rated film in Paris!"

"They got R-rated films there?"

"All their films are R-rated there. Commercials, too. And billboards. Too bad you'll never be going!"

"They got Tyler Perry, too?"

"Of course not! They've got culture there. Not that that matters to you. You won't be going. Well, it's true isn't it?"

Monsieur Richard was also the track coach. He held all of his practices in the morning instead of the afternoon—even though no one was using the track in the afternoon. And each morning, at 6:00 AM on the dot, he'd pick out one student to race once around the track. Usually, he'd target the newest kid or the fattest kid or the sleepiest kid or Janae, the shot-putter.

"What? You're on the track team but afraid to race? You too scared to race an old man like me? You think you can't take a thirty-three-year-old? Fifty pushups says I can take you."

He'd taunt until the kid had to accept the challenge. When the race began, Monsieur Richard would immediately jump out to a ten-yard lead; then he would slow until the kid was just a couple of steps behind him; then he'd sprint ahead another ten yards; then slow until the kid almost caught him; then speed off again. He'd do this for three-quarters of the lap, slowing just enough to make the kid think that maybe he could catch him and all the while driving the pace up until the kid could barely breathe. In the last stretch, he would finally allow the kid to get even with him. Then he'd salute once and sprint off to the finish line. The kid would stumble and sputter to the end— and then Monsieur Richard would make the kid do fifty pushups for losing.

"Nice try," he'd say.

"Nice try" was his all-time favorite thing to say— just ahead of "Well it's true, isn't it." In fact, "nice try" was the reason that he became a teacher in the first place. He felt an inch taller every time he had a chance to say it to a student.

"Nice try" was also the reason that Monsieur Richard couldn't suppress a grin when he caught Erica Meddler unsupervised in the hallway, peeking into Mr. White's classroom.

"Miss Meddler," he said. "Not in class, I see."

Erica continued looking through the glass in the

door. "Neither are you," she pointed out.

"It's my planning period," said Monsieur Richard.

"So why aren't you planning, then?" asked Erica.

"I am planning. Want to know what I'm planning?" said Monsieur Richard. He paused to allow Erica to take the bait. She didn't. He continued. "I'm planning to take you straight to the office." He smiled at his cleverness.

"I got a pass," said Erica calmly.

"You have a pass to stare into Mr. White's room?"

"Yeah." She reached into her purse and produced the pass that John Doe had written her. She waved it once in the air and tried to slip it back into her purse, but Monsieur Richard caught her by the wrist and removed the pass from her clenched hand. He read it. "Nice try," he said. "The library's that way."

Erica rolled her eyes.

"But you, Miss Meddler, aren't going to the library, either." He took her by the elbow and began leading her to the main office. "We have procedures for cutters."

Erica told him to get his hands off her. He held on just another second and then dropped her elbow. He escorted her down the hallway, though, holding his arms stiffly out to the side and puffing out his chest. When they reached the main office, he swung the door so hard that it hit a student who was on his way out of the office with an armful of worksheets.

"Watch where you're going!" Monsieur Richard said. Then he turned to Ms. Noreen, who hadn't looked up from her book. "Where's Fehler?" he demanded. Ms. Noreen pointed to the closed door of the principal's office. "She busy?"

"Yes."

"How about Luney?"

Ms. Noreen pointed to the assistant principal's closed door, which was right next to the principal's.

"He busy?"

Ms. Noreen turned a page.

"Luney!" called Monsieur Richard. "Luney! You busy?"

Luney cracked the door, mumbled something incoherent, and then, several seconds later, appeared in the doorway, grinning from ear to ear. "Never too busy for Monsieur Richard. How are you? Having a lovely and productive day?"

"Caught this one cutting class."

"I have a pass," said Erica.

"She was cutting," said Monsieur Richard. "Erica Meddler is a known cutter, recalcitrant, and general nuisance."

"Now, now!" said Dr. Luney. "Keep it positive." He pointed to the sign on his door that said: *Attitudes are contagious. Is yours worth catching?*

"Well, it's true isn't it?" said Monsieur Richard. "She's a little shit and we all know it."

"But she has good aspects, too!" said Dr. Luney.

"Geez, man! I'm out there in the hall, doing your job for you. The least you could say is thanks." Monsieur Richard's pink head pulsed and tensed, revealing every blue vein from his shoulders to the tip top.

"Thanks?" asked Dr. Luney.

Monsieur Richard relaxed. "You're welcome. I'll leave her with you for now." Monsieur Richard gave her a nudge toward Dr. Luney's office, and Erica marched in. Monsieur Richard called after her, "And I'll see you at track practice tomorrow morning!"

Dr. Luney smiled and shook Monsieur Richard's

hand, leaving fingerprints. Monsieur stiff-armed his way out the door. Erica sat in Dr. Luney's chair and put her feet up on his desk.

12

Dr. Luney was everyone's favorite. It was hard work being everyone's favorite. But luckily for him, as assistant principal, it was the only work he had to do. And he was a natural at it, anyway. The key was to keep a smile on his face, a song in his heart, and a flask in his desk drawer.

"Luney, I swear to God, I'm gonna kill that man. He a fuckin' dickhead," said Erica.

"Oh, my goodness gracious sakes alive!" said Dr. Luney. "Be careful with your language, Little Scholar."

"Sorry. But you know it's true!" said Erica. "He a dick."

"He means well," said Dr. Luney.

"No," said Erica. "He a little white man on a power trip. Little white men on power trips be bad news."

Dr. Luney sat in the guest's chair, across the desk from Erica. He offered her a peppermint from the jar on the desktop. Erica declined.

"Dr. Luney, you gotta switch me outta his class," said Erica. "I already gotta see that man for track practice."

"It'd be easier if you quit track, instead" suggested Dr. Luney. "Then you would only see him once a day—and I wouldn't have to get involved."

"I'm fast," said Erica. "Gonna get me a scholarship to go to college."

"You have to pass your classes, too, Little Scholar."

"I know! That's why I need you to put me in with Mr. White."

"He teaches Japanese."

"Counts as a foreign language, right?"

"Yes," said Dr. Luney.

"Just like French," said Erica.

"And Spanish," added Dr. Luney.

Erica looked at him. "What's Spanish got to do with it?"

"It's also a foreign language," said Dr. Luney patiently. He had earned his Ph.D. online, concentrating on early childhood education. He knew the importance of pattern-recognition for cognitive development.

"I'm not taking Spanish!" said Erica. "They always be talking 'bout people." By they, Erica meant the Hispanic students, who were—not coincidentally—the only students who took Spanish. It raised the school's test scores.

"I'm not telling you to take Spanish," said Dr. Luney. "I'm telling you to stay in French. You don't want to throw away everything you learned in class so far this semester, do you?"

Erica shrugged. "I'm not going to France anyway. Why do I need French?"

"Maddy Okafor speaks French," pointed out Dr.

Luney.

"Maddy Okafor from Africa. Monsieur Richard says they don't speak real French in the Congo." Monsieur Richard had said that just after Maddy Okafor corrected his pronunciation and just before he put her out of his class for good. Maddy Okafor had been devastated because, up to that point, she had been on the honor roll.

Erica continued, "And they switched *her* to Mr. White's class."

Dr. Luney said that wasn't the point. And Erica asked what the point was. And Dr. Luney, who had forgotten his initial point said the first point that came to his mind, "The point is, she doesn't speak Japanese natively."

"*No one* speaks Japanese natively!" said Erica.

"Little Kimi Suzuki does," said Dr. Luney.

"Kimi Suzuki?" asked Erica. "The Chinese girl."

"Exactly," said Dr. Luney.

"So I can take Japanese?" Erica asked.

But Dr. Luney explained that she hadn't understood his point. Not to mention she'd be behind in Japanese.

"Don't worry 'bout that. I've been auditing Mr. White's class."

"You've what?"

"I've been auditing."

"What do you mean you've been auditing?"

What Erica Meddler meant was that she had been staring into his classroom window at every opportunity she had. Mr. White had chocolate milky skin and big brown eyes and perfect skinny dreadlocks. He wore tight jeans and tight shirts and half sat on the front of his desk when he taught, partially supporting himself with fully-flexed arms. Every girl in his class audited him carefully, though they never heard a word he said. Every boy in class measured him up, wondering why someone hadn't already beaten him up. The general consensus was that he must be certifiably crazy. No black man could be as pretentious as he and not get beaten up unless he was completely crazy. You don't fuck with crazy.

So, while the girls audited, the boys fake-coughed "gay" into their fists—never realizing that the real reason Mr. White had never been beaten up was that he was from the suburbs of Portland and had been the least pretentious person in town.

"I mean," said Erica, "I been auditing."

"But—"

Dr. Luney's Walkie Talkie coughed at him. Then Principal Fehler's voice sputtered out. "LUNEY! LUNEY! COME IN, LUNEY!" she said.

Dr. Luney held up one finger to Erica, took a swig from his water bottle, cleared his throat, and then picked up the Walkie Talkie. "I'm with a student right now."

"WHAT?"

"I'm with a student right now," he said, keeping his voice light but clutching the device with a white-knuckled grip.

"WHAT DO YOU MEAN YOU'RE WITH A STUDENT?"

"I have a student in the office."

"WHO?"

"Erica Meddler."

Pause. Dr. Luney exhaled slowly, took a sip from his bottle, and set the Walkie Talkie on the desk. He smiled at Erica. "So, you were saying something about aud—"

"PUT ERICA ON."

Dr. Luney's eye twitched, but he kept a smile on his face. "I'm sorry?"

"PUT ERICA ON."

"Come again?"

"PUT ERICA MEDDLER ON THE WALKIE TALKIE!"

Erica held her hand out.

"ERICA!"

Dr. Luney passed the phone to Erica, a little more forcefully than he intended. Erica held the Walkie Talkie between her shoulder and ear and massaged her palm.

"ERICA! I NEED YOU TO COME TO MY OFFICE!"

"Fine," said Erica. She passed the Walkie Talkie back to Dr. Luney.

"Thanks!" Dr. Luney began. "Have a fantastic 405—"

"OVER!" said Principal Fehler, and it was.

Erica stood to go. "Anyway, you gonna switch me to Mr. White's class?" Erica asked.

"I would," said Dr. Luney, "But I'm not the one that does the scheduling. Ms. Morose does that."

"She do?"

"She do," Dr. Luney smiled and stood as well.

"God dammit," said Erica.

She walked past Dr. Luney on her way out the door. He stood and gave her a quick thump on the back that nearly took her breath away. "Keep it positive, Little Scholar. Be good! You can just talk to Ms. Morose when she gets back."

"Nah," she said. "I'll take care of things on my

own." Erica didn't have time to wait for Ms. Morose. "Thanks anyway!" she said.

13

Ms. Morose was the most dedicated guidance counselor in the City. Even though, technically, she hadn't actually been in the City for three weeks. Her absence, though, was only because she was committed to the reform movement.

When she was first hired, her role was straightforward and monotonous: she helped students select classes and fed them peanut butter crackers when they acted up in class. With the reform movement, however, there were so few electives that scheduling wasn't really a full-time job. So the Department of Achievement and Accountability gave her an additional role: Attendance Monitor.

"What does that entail?" asked Ms. Morose when Mr. Jankins of the Department of Achievement and Accountability called her and informed her of her additional task.

"Nothing much," said Mr. Jankins. "Just tracking attendance, reporting any trends, retrieving truant students, and maintaining the federally mandated 92% daily attendance rate."

"I'm responsible for the attendance rate?"

"Of course. Someone has to be held accountable. And you can't say it's the student's fault for being absent, can you?"

Ms. Morose knew that that was something you could only *think*.

"Of course you can't! Imagine how that would go over! So, instead, *you'll* be held accountable. You'll do great, though!" And with that, Mr. Jankins hung up the phone.

And so Ms. Morose went about trying to improve the attendance rate. She tried phone calls, but had mostly bad numbers. She tried one house visit, but chickened out right before knocking on Dontay Peterson's front door, when she heard a woman inside yell, "Who ate the last of the mother-fucking Captain Crunch? I'ma fuck someone up!" She tried incentive programs for perfect attendance: surprise field trips, bonus bucks, and perfect attendance raffles for a bicycle, a Pizza Hut gift certificate, and an iPod mini. But they didn't work. The dates of the surprise field trips got leaked to the students—so everyone, even the truant kids and a few who weren't enrolled, made it to school that day; the bonus bucks were copied, so the school store quickly ran out of markers and pens (and the bathroom stalls quickly got out of control); and all the raffles were somehow won by Breyona Phillips, who only made it thirteen feet off school property before forfeiting her booty to the angry masses. Except the Pizza Hut gift certificate. Pizza Hut wouldn't deliver to most City neighborhoods anyway.

After her initial ideas failed, Ms. Morose came up with an even better plan: she would hold the teachers accountable for their own attendance.

And so it was that the teachers, then, tried phone

calls and one home visit and incentives. But attendance still didn't go up. Worse, Ms. Eagleton started coming around, whining.

"Why are we being held responsible for attendance?"

"Well, you can't hold the kids responsible for their own attendance, can you?"

"Yes."

Ms. Morose frowned because Ms. Eagleton wasn't supposed to say that aloud.

"They're minors. It's the law."

"My students are mostly seventeen, can't we just remove them from the roster?"

Ms. Morose made a phone call.

"No!" explained Mr. Jankins, "You can't remove them from the roster unless you have proof that they are enrolled in another school. The Achievement and Accountability Department has to improve its dropout rate!"

"But these kids have never even been to class! Our attendance rate can't improve unless we remove the students who have dropped out."

"No one said achievement would be easy!" said Mr. Jankins. "This is reform! If you want them off your records, you'll have to convince them to transfer. You could try School 406." School 406 was the only other neighborhood high school left. School 404 had been completely shut down. And Schools 401-403 had been transformed into charter schools (Martin Academy, Luther Academy, and King Academy), so they no longer had to accept transfer students.

Ms. Morose explained the situation to Ms. Eagleton. "Look, if you want the students who do not attend your class off your roster, you'll have to convince them to sign papers to not-attend at another school."

"How can I get them to sign transfer papers if they don't come to school?"

"Try to find them?"

"Try to find them? Look at this first one: Juan Alamarez. He went back to Mexico. Just my luck!" This sort of thing always happened to Ms. Eagleton. "His mother gets deported and he decides to follow her back without even signing the papers! I'm so unlucky! Can't you do anything?"

Ms. Morose made a phone call.

"He moved to a new city?" asked Mr. Jankins.

"Yes, Mexico."

"Mexico's not a city, Ms. Morose."

"A new country then."

"Do you have his immigration papers?"

"To Mexico?"

"Yes."

"No. He was undocumented. There were no papers to begin with."

"How did he enroll if there were not papers?"

"He put down his name and address."

"So there *were* papers."

"We had his name and current address."

"A City address?"

"A City address."

"So you can find him."

"He doesn't live there anymore."

"You said it was current."

"It's not anymore."

"So you don't have his current address?"

"Not currently."

"So how do you know he went back to Mexico?"

"Facebook."

Mr. Jankins looked at the list of approved proofs of address. "Facebook does not qualify as official documentation. He'll have to remain on your roster until you can officially prove that he has officially transferred to a new school in a new city."

Ms. Morose explained the situation to Ms. Eagleton. "We need a current current address to prove our current address isn't current."

Ms. Eagleton frowned. "Just my luck."

Ms. Morose nodded.

"Well," said Ms. Eagleton. "What now?"

Ms. Morose thought the situation over very carefully. And then she had her most brilliant idea yet. "I'll take care of it," she said.

She packed the transfer papers and her swimming suit and booked a flight to Cancun on the school's expense account. The students would have to do without peanut butter crackers for the next ten years—but if they were really hungry, they could always lift something from Don's or something. And nourishing the children wasn't her priority anyway. Attendance was. And she'd find Juan Alamarez, even if it took her the rest of the year. In the meantime, she'd instructed Dr. Luney to throw out the teacher's attendance records and mark everyone besides Juan present—as a temporary accountability measure. The Department of Achievement and Accountability commended her efforts and mailed her a purple ribbon for attendance improvement.

"Just my luck!" said Ms. Eagleton. She had been so close to escape.

14

It wasn't the only time that Ms. Eagleton had been close to escape. In fact, just a month before John Doe showed up at 405, she had been steps away from permanent freedom.

It had been just her luck that Jazmine Williams, who had never before shown up for a detention, picked that afternoon, the very afternoon that could have changed Ms. Eagleton's life—to saunter in, popping her gum.

"Well?" said Jazmine.

"Well?" said Ms. Eagleton.

"I'm here."

"I see that."

"Should I just sit or what?"

Ms. Eagleton hesitated a moment. She couldn't just let Jazmine walk out, but she also didn't have much time before the post office closed. Why don't you pick up the trash on the floor? Then you can leave."

Jazmine examined the littered tiled floor. "I'm not a janitor. And I know my rights." She took a seat in the back of the classroom. "How long I gotta be here?"

"Until I say," said Ms. Eagleton.

Jazmine shrugged and put her head on the desk. Ms. Eagleton looked at the clock. She could at least save some time by making the address label there in the classroom. Ms. Eagleton took a glance at Jazmine and then turned on her classroom computer.

Upon hearing the machine clank to life, Jazmine lifted her head.

"Can I use that?"

"No."

Jazmine's head went back down. Ms. Eagleton logged onto her eBay account to double-check the buyer's address. She wrote it neatly on a sheet of paper. Then she carefully slipped the book out of her desk. It didn't fit in her teacher bag, so she just placed the book next to her bag. Not that she was likely to forget it.

"What's that?" Jazmine asked.

"A book," Ms. Eagleton said.

"Looks old. What book?" Jazmine asked.

"Just some old poems," Ms. Eagleton said.

"Sounds boring," said Jazmine.

Typical. Ms. Eagleton shook her head at Jazmine's cultural ignorance. *Tamerlane and Other Poems* was an extremely valuable book. Ms. Eagleton knew from *Antiques Roadshow*. She had seen this same rare edition go for $450,000. And *she* had received an offer for even more that day on eBay. Enough that she would never have to darken the doorway of room 204, or any other classroom, again.

"I like poems, though," said Jazmine, standing and starting toward Ms. Eagleton.

Ms. Eagleton protectively covered the fragile

book. This book was Ms. Eagleton's treasure: she'd found it fair and square—while avoiding City Teacher Union Representative Aliyah Deere, SCS, SC, BHCO, JSC, who was trying to sell her cookie dough for the National Honor Society. City Teacher Union Representative Aliyah Deere, SCS, SC, BHCO, JSC, was the faculty advisor for National Honor Society (NHSFA), too. Ms. Eagleton had been ducking down behind a shelf when she spotted the precious book.

Ms. Eagleton frowned at the approaching student. With her luck, Jazmine would smack spittle all over her ticket to freedom. Ms. Eagleton considered grabbing the book and running out of the room, but that might raise suspicion. She scrambled for a solution. But luckily, Jazmine was distracted by a dust-covered umbrella that some student must have left on the floor.

"This yours?" she asked.

"No," said Ms. Eagleton.

Jazmine tucked the disgusting thing under her arm. Ms. Eagleton covered her mouth to hide a smirk. Jazmine cared more about trash than treasure. It confirmed her theory. No one would miss the book. No one in the whole school could appreciate it. They would just think it was old, ugly, and boring. They couldn't see its deeper value like Ms. Eagleton could.

"Okay," Ms. Eagleton said. "You can go."

"That count for all seven of them?"

"Sure," said Ms. Eagleton, gathering her belongings.

The two headed for the main entrance, Ms. Eagleton carrying the book in the arm farthest from Jazmine. As they were about cross the door's threshold, there was a clap of thunder. Then a downpour.

Ms. Eagleton stopped, shocked. Jazmine opened the umbrella and sauntered away. "Bye, Ms. Eagleton"

"Wait, Jazmine!" Ms. Eagleton said, reaching for her arm. "Can you walk me to my—"

But of course, Jazmine didn't stop.

Just her luck. Ms. Eagleton shook her head at Jazmine's nerve. The umbrella wasn't even hers. Then she searched around the lobby for something waterproof that she could use to protect the book. She was pulling a trash bag out of an empty trash bin when Mrs. Brown came up from behind her.

"Excuse me, Ms. Eagleton!" she said. "Is that a library book?" She held out her hand. Ms. Eagleton clutched the precious book to her chest. "What book?"

"Stealing is a prosecutable offense, you know," said Mrs. Brown.

"I'm just checking it out," said Ms. Eagleton.

"The checkout desk is upstairs. And what do you need a poetry book for?" she asked. "You teach math."

"For fun," she said.

Ms. Brown frowned. "Well, this one's no longer in circulation she said."

"But—"

Mrs. Brown narrowed her eyes. Ms. Eagleton sighed and surrendered the property. She watched Ms. Brown carry the book away.

Just her luck, she thought. She kicked the trashcan over, but then she saw Janitor Bob, who was sweeping the hallway, tilt his head at her. She apologized to Janitor Bob by saying that the trashcan was empty anyway. Then she picked it up and started out the door—

only to be intercepted by City Teacher Union Representative Aliyah Deere, SCS, SC, BHCO, JSC, NHSFA.

"I know I can count on you to buy some cookie dough!" said City Teacher Union Representative Aliyah Deere, SCS, SC, BHCO, JSC, NHSFA.

15

Janitor Bob had tilted his head at Ms. Eagleton's antics, but he hadn't been surprised. If only he had a nickel for every knocked over trashcan, he thought. And then he stretched his back and gripped his broom and began down the hallway.

If he had a nickel for every trashcan he picked up and every pencil stub he swept up, he thought, for every pencil stub and every pen cap, too, he added as his legs swish-swished and his broom, a 24-inch Kwickie Pusher, scraped across the littered floor. He'd asked Principal Fehler for the 30-inch Super Sweep, but she said she just couldn't fit it in the budget; he'd have to save up for it himself. His knock-off broom—no substitute for the real thing but the real thing, he always said—scraped along, allowing the smaller bits to squeeze through the bristles.

If he only had a nickel, he thought, for every crumpled bit of paper and every chunk of dried-up gum and every candy wrapper and empty plastic bottle; if he just had a nickel for them and the pieces of chalk and the Tic Tacs and the paper cones for water and the sunflower seed shells—oh! the sunflower seed shells—and one for every shoe lace and pencil shaving and chip bag and index card and glue stick cap and marker cap and baseball cap, and one for every broken umbrella and missing glove and crunched-up staple and warped paperclip and broken paperclip and dropped paperclip, just a nickel for each torn shirt or ripped out weave or used Band-Aid; if he just had a nickel for every bit and piece he swept, thought Janitor Bob as he swish-swish-swished down the long empty hallway with his 24-inch Kwickie Pusher—

Then he reached the end of the hallway and shook out his broom, depositing the scraps from the school day in an uneven pile. In the middle of the pile, something shiny caught his eye. He stooped and picked it up—a nickel. He put it in his front pocket, his Super Sweep fund. Only $36.24 to go. Then he started swish-swish-swishing back the other direction.

If he only had a nickel for every pop can, he thought as his broom scraped across the littered tiled floor—

16

"Fehler wants to see you in her office," Erica yelled through the open classroom door, stirring John Doe from his stupor. No one had shown up for Ms. Alloway's second period class, so he had just been staring at the clock, allowing his thoughts to roam, unchecked.

"Fehler?"

"Principal Fehler," said Erica, chomping on a Cheezy Ball that she had withdrawn from a paper cone.

"What does Principal Fehler want?" asked John Doe.

"That's what you go to the office for," Erica said. "To find out."

John Doe hesitated. "But the classroom," he said. "Should I just leave it unattended?"

"I'll watch it for you," said Erica. "Run along!" John Doe stood, and Erica took his place at Ms. Alloway's chair, swinging her feet on top of the desk. "Hustle! She doesn't have all day!" Erica prodded with her best white lady impression.

"Principal Fehler?" John Doe asked when he

reached the main office. Ms. Noreen nodded her head toward Principal Fehler's open office door. John Doe went inside.

"Close the door!" demanded Principal Fehler.

He closed the door.

"Come in."

He was already in, so he just stood there. Principal Fehler scrutinized him. "Sit down." He sat.

Principal Fehler looked at John Doe. John Doe tried to look back at Principal Fehler, but he quickly realized that he could not do it without noticeably staring at the giant, orange-tinted mole on Principal Fehler's chin. It was disgusting. He focused on the items on her desk: pencil holder full of sharpened number two pencils, a *World's Best Principal* mug, and an oversized plastic jug of Cheezy Balls.

"I think you know why you're here," said Principal Fehler.

"Not really," said John Doe.

Principal Fehler narrowed her eyes but said nothing.

"Is it about the attendance sheet?"

"What attendance sheet?"

"The one from the classroom   where I was subbing."

"You took attendance, too?"

"I tried."

"What kind of sub are you?" Principal Fehler asked. She couldn't tell if John Doe was playing with her or playing against her. "I understand that you were trying to teach, too. Reading to the children instead of letting them proceed with test preparation. Don't deny it!" She gave him time to deny it.

"Look," said John Doe, "I think there's been some

mistake."

"Oh, there's no mistake. I have good information."

"No, I mean—"

"There's no mistake!"

John Doe glanced at the mole and then looked back at the desk. Principal Fehler followed his eyes.

"You see, I have a mole," she said. "I have moles all over, of course. But one mole, in particular, that has been the source of, shall we say, an interesting tidbit."

"You might want to get that checked out," said John Doe. "Moles can be dangerous if you let them get out of hand."

"I don't need to check anything out!" said Principal Fehler. "I just need a straight answer from you."

"I'm not an expert or anything," said John Doe.

"I should say not. You don't seem to have the first clue as to what you are doing." She narrowed her eyes. "Well?" she said. "Are you going to give me a straight answer?"

"If I were you, I'd just try to cover it up."

Principal Fehler narrowed her eyes further. In fact, they were awfully close to completely shut.

"What, exactly, are you suggesting?"

"I just think there might be ways to make it less noticeable."

"I didn't realize I was drawing extra attention."

"A Band-Aid might work."

Principal Fehler stroked her chin. "I'm not sure I know what you mean."

"A Band-Aid. You know." John Doe fished around his pockets to see if he had any extra, but he couldn't put his hands on one. He shrugged. "You know. A Band-Aid."

Principal Fehler frowned. "I don't have time to get cute."

John Doe pointed out that it didn't take long to put on a Band-Aid. There were bunches of Band-Aids on South Avenue. She might want to keep some Band-Aids here, too.

"What do you know about Band-Aids on South Ave.?" asked Principal Fehler.

"Well, I work there. In the Office formerly known as Human Resources," he said.

"So you're not really a sub?"

"No."

Principal Fehler finally just shut her eyes. "Why are you telling me all this?" she asked. "What's in it for you?"

"For me? I just want to see your good side, I guess."

"My good side?" she opened her eyes and stroked her chin, brushing her fingernails over the disgusting facial feature. He couldn't look her in the eye. He glanced away, toward the Cheezy Balls. "I see," said Principal Fehler. "I assume you'll be attending the faculty meeting today."

"I wasn't planning on it—"

"Well, change your plans. I could use someone like you. You see, the time has come for me to put on my game face, and I need to know how the teachers react."

"You mean, you want me to see if they say anything about your, uh, game face behind your back?"

"Precisely. I need things to be perfect. This is do-or-die time."

"Is it really that important? I mean, in the grand

scheme of things, a little blemish isn't so bad."

"*A little blemish* is the difference between Principal Fehler and Chancellor Fehler! Listen, I just need to know if you notice any *blemishes* at the faculty meeting."

"Well, if you think it's that important——"

Principal Fehler slapped her open hand on the desk. Then she took a deep breath. "I pamper my moles, you know."

"Pamper them? With what?"

"I thought you had already figured that out." Principal Fehler retrieved a paper cone and filled it with Cheezy Balls. She handed it to John Doe. "These aren't just to satisfy my personal cravings, you know."

"I see," said John Doe, "That explains a lot."

17

Ms. Young, level one consultant for UCAN edUCA-tioN, fake-smiled at the sorry lot in front of her while Principal Fehler finished up the general announcements in her characteristic style, wavering in volume between the level she used to be threatening in person and the level she used to be threatening over the announcements:

"—because YOU set the TONE for your students! So if you're SAYING, 'Waaah, the classroom is HOT,' or 'EW, a roach!' or 'YES, this school is a dirty, DIRTY hellhole,' then you can only expect that THEY will REPEAT it! And we DON'T want to give that sort of IMPRESSION if we have GUESTS from South Avenue. Between the NEGATIVE attitudes and the prevalent HOODIES, it's a wonder they haven't already shut us down!"

"But the school is a dirty, dirty hellhole," muttered Monsieur Richard, who was sitting at the back, next to John Doe and Dr. Luney—and wearing a hoodie. A few members of the sorry lot sniggered, but most (though they agreed) rolled their eyes. Monsieur Richard was a dickhead.

Principal Fehler frowned, so Ms. Young frowned, too.

"Did you HAVE something to say, Monsieur Richard?"

Ms. Young nodded her head.

"No, Fuhrer!" said Monsieur Richard.

Principal Fehler continued. "That's EXACTLY the ATTITUDE I'm talking about! You're not making this place feel inviting and HOMEY. You're making it sound WORSE than some of these kids' OWN homes!"

Silence.

"Finally, as you know, our school has been listed as *At Risk* for closure. We obviously do NOT want this to happen. Keep in mind that YOU will be held accountable if your scores do not go up this MAY. It's all about the STATE EXAMS. As such, I have arranged for one last session of PROFESSIONAL development. And if, after all this, your scores don't go up, you won't be able to BLAME ME. Have I not reminded you EVERY DAY that the STATE EXAMS are coming? Have I not given you EVERY RESOURCE available? You have NO ONE to blame but yourselves if you fail. Keep that in mind."

Sensing that her time to shine had come, Ms. Young stepped forward. But before she could say anything, Principal Fehler added, "Now, before we get to YOUR professional DEVELOPMENT, Ms. Noreen has an ANNOUNCEMENT to make." Ms. Young stepped back.

Ms. Noreen, who was sitting at the back of the library to prevent teachers from escaping early, set down her book and stood. "Copy machine's broken," she said. "Due to overuse. From now on, all copies will have to be approved and made by me. There will be a new password." She sat back down. "I'll be the only one who knows it."

"THANK you, Ms. Noreen," said Principal Fehler. Ms. Young stepped forward. "If you ABUSE privileges, they get taken AWAY!" Ms. Young stepped back. Principal Fehler continued. "With THAT in mind, please welcome UCAN consultant Ms. Michelle Young." Ms. Young stepped forward. "AFTER one last announcement," Principal Fehler said. "Dr. Luney?"

Dr. Luney stood. But as soon as he stood, he forgot what he had to say. "I just wanted to tell you all, keep up the terrific work," he said, tapping his pen on the table so enthusiastically that the top broke off. He started to sit, and Ms. Young stepped forward, and then he remembered what he was going to say, "Oh! And we have a birthday today! Mr. White! Go ahead, stand up."

Mr. White stood and flashed a panty-dropping smile. The women of the sorry lot grinned back and re-crossed their legs—as did Mr. Priddy, the closeted soccer coach. The men sucked in and straightened their backs and tried (unsuccessfully) to make their shoulders as broad as Mr. White's.

"Happy Birthday!" said Dr. Luney.

"Thanks!" said Mr. White in his rich baritone. "In Japan, they'd say, 'Otanjōbiomedetōgozaimasu.'" Mr. White winked at the nearest lady. "I spent some time in Tokyo after college." Monsieur Richard fake-coughed "gay" into his hand.

"It's Ms. Villanueva's birthday, too," Mr. Howard pointed out.

"Oh, of course," Dr. Luney said. He looked toward the table of Filipino teachers, unsure which one was Ms. Villanueva. Each year, City Schools recruited, imported, and emergency-certified a dozen teachers from the Philippines—in addition to the troop of well-meaning but breakdown-prone Liberal Arts graduates—to fill in shortages in the Special Ed and Math departments. But the Filipinos were just so hard to tell apart. One woman at the table stood up. "Happy Birthday!" said Dr. Luney to her, though it was actually Ms. Cruz who stood up—needing to use the restroom.

"I flew through the Philippines on my way back from Japan," said Mr. White. "The second time, anyway."

"Great!" said Dr. Luney. "Well, that's all the announcements I have. Principal Fehler, back to you!"

"HAPPY birthday to ALL!" said Principal Fehler, managing to keep all goodwill out of her voice. "IT is without FURTHER ADO—since you all always COMPLAIN about how long these meetings are, even though they are for your own GOOD. ANYWAY, it is without FURTHER ADO that I will turn things over to Ms. YOUNG, level one consultant for UCAN education, our CONSULTING partner. SHE has been working with the Department of ACHIEVEMENT AND ACCOUNTABILITY to develop more TOOLS for ACHIEVEMENT for you all." Ms. Young stepped forward. "UNLESS there are FURTHER ANNOUNCEMENTS." Ms. Young stepped back. No one spoke. Principal Fehler scanned the room for a moment. Ms. Young stepped forward.

"Oh!" said City Teacher Union Representative Aliyah Deere, SCS, SC, BHCO, JSC, NHSFA, standing suddenly, "The foreign language club is selling

Bon Bons." City Teacher Union Representative Aliyah Deere, SCS, SC, BHCO, JSC, NHSFA, was also
the Foreign Language Club Facilitator (FLCF.)
"Please support us as we raise funds to visit China-
town."

City Teacher Union Representative Aliyah Deere
SCS, SC, BHCO, JSC, NHSFA, FLCF, sat down.
Ms. Young hesitated. Principal Fehler turned to her,
"Go on, then. We haven't got all day!"

Ms. Young stepped forward and clapped her
hands enthusiastically. The sorry lot just stared at her.

"Thank you so much, Principal Fehler, for inviting
me to your fine establishment's faculty meeting. My
name is Ms. Young, and I am a special consultant for
UCAN edUCAtioN—a group that helps put the
UCAN back into education."

Some members of the sorry lot took notes. Others
doodled on their agendas, or rolled their eyes, checked
their phones, or just sort of stared with glazed-over
eyes at the mostly empty library shelves, which had
been shifted around to create space for the faculty
meeting.

"I am very excited to be here. You all may not
know this, but School 405 is where I got my start in
the wonderful journey of education."

The sorry lot knew. Ms. Young had taught at 405
just last year.

"As such, you should understand that I know
EXACTLY what you all are going through." Ms.
Young consciously imitated Principal Fehler's effective
emphasis practices. "This TIME of the year, as we
near the State Exams, is both stressful and EXHILA-
RATING."

Silence. She tried a different tact.

"Anyway, I know that test prep sometimes has a negative connotation, right? Like how many times can you say, 'Process of Elimination,' right? Or 'If all else fails, pick *C*?' It gets old, huh?" She paused. "Am I right?"

The sorry lot gripped their red pens a little tighter.

"Well, lucky for you, test prep analytics, or TPA as we call it at UCAN, have moved beyond those two, outdated pieces of advice. TPA is now advanced enough that we know that *C* is not *always* the best letter to guess. In fact, the most recent studies have identified a much more common pattern across all test-making answer generators."

Ms. Young paused for dramatic effect. The sorry lot raised their sorry eyes.

"It is: DACCBCCABD. Got it? Say it with me! DACCBCCABD."

A few members of the sorry lot, mostly first year teachers, half-heartedly stumbled along.

"OK!" said Ms. Young. "You guys are so smart! Now let's do it one more time. All together now!"

Mr. Howard, who had been fighting to control his anger and restrain his tears ran out of energy. "What?" he asked. "WHAT IS THIS?"

"DACCBCCABD!" said Ms. Young. "I can do it slower, though, if you like—"

"No, I mean, what, exactly, are we supposed to do with those letters?"

Ms. Young's fake smile grew even faker, reaching all the way up to her eyes. She spoke slowly so that Mr. Howard could understand her. "Those letters are the most common answer pattern that advanced TPA has identified for multiple-choice tests with four answer options. Now in states where the exam has alternating choices of ABCD and then EFGH, it gets a lit-tle trickier—as do the ones where there are five choic-es. But for our intensive purposes, this is the pattern that we will be focusing on."

"Isn't that cheating?" he interrupted, unable to keep a single tear from rolling down his cheek.

Ms. Young went wide-eyed at the accusation, and Principal Fehler went narrow-eyed, and the sorry lot ping-ponged their eyes from Ms. Young to Mr. How-ard.

"Cheating?"

"You're telling them which answers to pick."

"This is analytics! It's no different than telling them to just guess C, if they don't know. This is just the data-driven next step. It's just a more advanced test-taking tip!"

"It's a tool for your TEACHING TOOLBELT!" said Principal Fehler. "You can't BLAME ME for test scores. I'm giving YOU tools!"

"But it has nothing to do with assessing knowledge," said Mr. Howard. By this time, his chest was heaving so hard that he could barely choke the words out. No one could make eye-contact with him. It was too awkward.

"Oh," said Ms. Young, forcing her smile to the edges of her ears but looking at the shelves behind Mr. Howard, "We have moved beyond that long ago. Re-search tells us that multiple-choice exams are not valid assessments of knowledge, indicators of aptitude, or predictors of future success. They even made the SATs change their name from Scholastic Aptitude Test to just SAT."

The sorry lot collectively blinked.

Ms. Young smiled patiently at their ignorance.

They needed an analogy. "It's like how KFC no longer stands for Kentucky Fried Chicken," she began, trying to find something that these teachers might be able to comprehend, "Because their chicken isn't really chickeny enough to—"

"Why are we giving the tests, then?" Mr. Howard managed to sputter.

"Oh!" said Ms. Young. "For accountability, of course. Someone's got to be held accountable for our children's education. And you certainly don't want it to be you!"

Mr. Howard wanted to argue but only gurgled a little.

Ms. Young continued. "Anyway, so far, eleven schools across the country are using UCAN TPA techniques. And to great success! Ten of them have been named *Blue Ribbon Schools* and the other one received the *Most Improved School in the State* award. That's why the Department of Achievement and Accountability sought us out. This method is really all the rage!"

"It's ALL the rage!" repeated Principal Fehler, who was desperately trying to get Ms. Noreen's attention. "THE RAGE!" she yelled. Ms. Noreen turned a page from the book. Principal Fehler finally just walked to the back and whispered something in her ear. Ms. Noreen rolled her eyes, tucked her book under her right arm, and walked out of the room.

"And the coolest thing about it," said Ms. Young, "Is that we just received enough money through a generous donation to provide necessary support materials!" She waited for the gasp of excitement. It didn't happen. "Like T-shirts!"

"Free ones?" asked Ms. Eagleton.

"Yes!"

A few teachers nodded at that. Ms. Young went on. "And the even cooler coolest thing is that there's a creative element to it. Check it out!" Ms. Young pushed a button, and loud, fuzzy music blasted from a boom box. Then she flipped over the first page of her chart paper to reveal big block letters that said: *SCHOOL 405 – PERSONALIZED PNEUMONIC DE-VICE!* And then it listed the letters, *DACCBCCABD*, vertically down the side of the page. She turned off the music. "Woke you all up, huh?"

"Mnemonic is not spelled that way," said Mr. Howard as a few more tears squirted out.

"Oh!" said Ms. Young. "The P is silent. Common mistake!"

Mr. Howard might have replied, but he was cut off by an announcement from the overhead speakers. Mrs. Noreen's voice said: "Attention, Mr. Howard, there's an angry black woman on the line who would like to speak to you. Please report to the office immediately."

The dam broke, and the tears rushed out.

"Well?" said Principal Fehler.

Mr. Howard tried to say something, but the words were drowned in his flood of tears. After a moment of blubbering, he turned and left.

"He really hates faculty meetings," whispered Dr. Luney to John Doe.

"So," continued Ms. Young, "What I want all of you to do is to think of the perfect pneumonic device for your school. I'll pass out the sticky notes!"

18

Ms. Noreen shook her head at Mr. Howard, who had only partially composed himself, and handed him the phone. "Who is it?" Mr. Howard mouthed, but Ms. Noreen pretended not to notice. She put away her Rolodex and picked up her book.

"Hello?" said Mr. Howard.

"Hello!" said an angry black woman.

There was a pause. "Well?" she said. "What's he done this time? I don't got all day, you know."

"With whom am I speaking?" asked Mr. Howard.

"What do you mean with whom are you speaking? You're speaking to the person you called. Speaking of, don't you think you could find a better time to call than 4.30 in the afternoon?"

"I think—"

"A person gotta sleep sometime."

"But—"

"Right, the world revolves around you, of course. Well, go on, then."

Mr. Howard cleared his throat. "So, this is the parent or guardian of—"

"Dontay Peterson!" she said. "For fuck's sake. You

got something to say to me or not?"

"Well, actually, Dontay has been absent for the past week."

Silence.

"That it?" she said.

"Well, it's affecting his schoolwork."

"I'd sure as hell hope it affecting his schoolwork. Otherwise you ain't teaching much."

"Do you think you could encourage him to come to school, maybe?"

"Me? I ain't seen him."

"You haven't seen him."

"No, I *haven't* seen him," she said. "I work two jobs just tryin' to keep food on the table. Some of us work, you know."

Mr. Howard could feel the tears coming again. "I work, too," he said defensively.

"Well, you ain't very good at your job if you can't even keep track of your students."

"How am I supposed to keep track of him?" asked Mr. Howard.

"I might ask the same thing."

"Well—" said Mr. Howard.

"Listen. I be workin' sixteen hours a day. Sixteen hours a day tryin' to put food on the table."

"I understand," began Mr. Howard. "But—"

"You understand?" she asked. "You spend your day wiping and kissing asses at two different homes? Washin' shit outta yo' fingernails while listening to old white folks go on 'bout they grandchildren an' insect collections an' some shit?"

Mr. Howard did not.

"Yo' kids running around with gangbangers? You get woke up at 4:30 by some teacher who judgin' you 'cause your grown-ass kid acting a fool? Huh? You a black lady who got some white guy callin' you and sayin' he know what you're going through? Some white guy thinkin' you just another one of them angry black women that can't take care of her kids? Don't have her shit together?"

"Not exactly," said Mr. Howard, sniveling a little.

"So don't say you understand if you don't understand. Understand?"

"I think so."

"What do you mean you think so? It's a simple question. Do you or don't you?"

Mr. Howard whimpered in response.

"You cryin'?"

He was.

"God dammit," said Dontay's mom as she felt compelled to transfer from angry black woman to calloused, tough-love nanny. Did she only exist for the service and amusement of white folks? Was she just another flat, black specimen, drying out between white pages? "Now you be makin' a fuss and forcin' me into play a new role, huh? You whiney little—"

"I'm sorry! I'm so so sorry. For ... " Mr. Howard stuttered, trying to think of a way to apologize for the things he was responsible for but didn't understand. "...for everything." He sobbed loudly.

Dontay's mom couldn't take it. "Listen, you seem like you havin' a rough day." She paused. "I know you be tryin', Mister. But you not from here, you know?"

Mr. Howard knew.

"Let me tell you something, Little Man. You can't let things get to you, you hear?"

Mr. Howard inhaled slowly.

"I asked if you heard me," said the woman.

"I heard you," he said quietly.

"You gotta take care of yourself before you can save the world, you know. And it sound like you ain't been doing that good a job taking care of yourself."

Mr. Howard thought about it. He wiped his eyes with the back of his hand. "Yeah?"

"What do you mean, yeah? Of course, yeah! This type of world always goin' be trying to get you down. Always somethin'. But like the Poet said, 'they may trod you in the fuckin' dirt, but still, like dust, you rise!'"

"Who said that?"

"Point is, I want you to hang up this phone and do a little self-reflecting. I want you to think 'bout what it is you need. 'Cause, believe me, you need somethin'. You sound like you be one 'fuck off' from a complete fuckin' breakdown, you know what I mean? One missed bus, one empty cereal box, one spilt coffee, one dirty look away from complete meltdown. You know?"

Mr. Howard thought he knew.

"So here's what we goin' do. You goin' let that grown-ass kid be grown. Me, I'm goin' work. An' you, you goin' go on home an' take care of your own self, you see?"

"That sounds good," said Mr. Howard, wiping his nose.

"An' you decide you need to call again, for fuck's sake, pick a better time than 4.30 in the afternoon!"

"Yes ma'am."

Pause.

"Well?" said the woman. "You got anything else to say or you just waitin' for me to tell you 'have a blessed day?' 'Cause let me tell you somethin', Little

Man, I ain't sayin' it."

She hung up. Mr. Howard gave the phone back to Ms. Noreen, who accepted it tentatively, with two fingers. "You can use a Kleenex, like a grownup," she said. "You are even worse than the kids."

Mr. Howard's lip quivered.

"Well," continued Ms. Noreen, "When's the kid coming back?"

"She didn't know.

Ms. Noreen rolled her eyes. "Great. You know he stole a mega bottle of Cheezy Balls off Principal Fehler's desk."

"Are you sure?"

"Of course, I'm sure! We have it on tape. Five bottles of water from her fridge, too. Left the pea soup, though. God knows what went through that kid's mind."

"Maybe he doesn't like pea soup."

"So where is the kid, then?"

"His mom didn't know," said Mr. Howard.

"Typical," said Ms. Noreen. "They never know where their kids are.

But the kid's mom did know where he was. The number for the prison collect call service had popped up on her phone yesterday. She calmly ignored it this time. She was tired. And, frankly, she didn't want to know how he'd gotten there this time.

19

The kid had, in fact, taken the scenic route. After walking out of Mr. Howard's class, he had to pass the main office before reaching the main exit. The door to the main office was open, as was the door to Principal Fehler's inner-office. He walked right past Ms. Noreen and put the booty in his backpack. Then he walked right back out of the office.

The kid walked out of the office and then out of the school. And then he kept right on going; past the teacher's parking lot; past the bus stop; past the bar where the teachers went to forget about their students; past his own street. He kept right on going; past the corner store where the Chinese man kept his goods behind bulletproof glass; past the Chicken Joint, where sweaty white men ran the register and sweaty Mexicans cooked the food; past the part of the park where black kids popped wheelies on undersized bicycles; past the part of the park that had the benches carved with penises and gang signs; past the part of the park where Mexicans played volleyball with soccer balls; past the part of the park where white guys in short jean shorts and vests walked on homemade tightropes;

past the part of the park where white women carrying spare water bottles and pepper spray ran and where policemen in parked cars conspicuously followed the kid with their eyes until he was out of sight.

He went past the entire park and eventually reached Main Street. To his right were familiar corners. There was Mr. W's Chinese Takeout, which also sold condoms and miracle boner pills; there were liquor stores and pawn shops; there were bus stops where stoned white people fell asleep standing up; there were people who loved him and hated him and dealt with him. He turned left, toward the Best Buy and the Target and the people who would be aware of his exact position at all times but wouldn't actually make eye contact.

And then he kept going, past the TGI Fridays; past the cafes where rich people sat outside eating things called tapas; past the small clothing stores with French names; past the designer hair salons. Then he turned right and went past another park, where there were no black kids popping wheelies, though there were two playing freeze tag with some Chinese and white kids—while their mothers and fathers and a couple of cops stood to the side, smiling. In this park, the white guys in vests read books and the women runners pushed fancy strollers and the penises and gang signs on the benches had been painted over. The white ladies smiled nervously and shifted not quite imperceptibly out of his way. The policemen frowned.

He walked through that park and made one more left turn so that directly across the street was the ramp up to City Bridge. The kid stepped onto the street without hesitating, even though the crossing signal was a red hand. He was clipped by an angry man on his

THE ALLOWAY FILES

cellphone, who had waited until the very last second to swerve. The angry man didn't apply the breaks, thinking he was teaching the kid a lesson. But it was a lesson the kid had already been taught.

The kid walked up the ramp, sweating now, especially under his backpack. But he kept going, maneuvering around slow crowds of Chinese tourists with their cameras and a school group of girls in pleated skirts and matching polos. He slid past a young couple posing happily and a large group of men and women in suits and black skirts, who were chattering importantly to one another. One of the men made eyecontact with the kid, and the kid looked down. The kid walked past New Balances and Crocs and boots and heels and flip flops—flip flops!—until he finally reached the first of two pillars that supported the famous City Bridge. Then, with a quick movement, he jumped onto the handrail, swung a leg over the protective chain link fence on the other side, and carefully lifted himself, up, over, and down the other side, a narrow steel beam on the outside of the bridge.

"Oh my God," said one of the suited men—and six phone cameras whipped his direction.

"Help! Officer, help! Oh my God!"

One pair of feet thumped down the bridge; then two pairs thumped back up. But the kid had made it across the narrow beam to the wide outermost beam that hovered hundreds of feet above the filthy water.

"Son, son, SON, son, son, SON … " said the officer.

"Oh my God!" said a woman.

"What do you think's in the bag?" a new voice asked. A crowd gathered. People walking both directions stopped, stared, shouted.

The kid sat down, letting his feet dangle over the water.

"He's gonna jump!" said a woman.

"What else would he do?"

"What's in the backpack? Do you see the backpack? Do you think it could be—"

"SON, son, son, SON! You can't go out there, son."

The kid didn't turn his shoulder. He sat on the edge of the bridge. He dangled his feet over the water.

"Jump! You can do it!"

"Shut up, asshole."

"What's in the backpack?"

"A body?"

"Don't be stupid."

"A bomb?"

"Son!" another cop said, "Son, SON, son! You have to come back, son."

"Go get him," said another. "Anything could be in that bag."

"Son, SON, SON, SON!"

The kid sat and dangled his feet and looked over the water.

"This is boring," said someone.

"Shut up, asshole."

"Don't jump! Think of your family."

"Think of God. He will help you through anything."

"What's the point, anyway. If he wants to jump, he should jump. What's it to you?"

"What's it to *you*?"

"Son, SON, son, son, SON, SON! It is against the law for you to be here."

"JUMP, JUMP, JUMP!"

"Shut up, asshole."

"Do you think it's a gun in the backpack?"

"Son! What's in the backpack, son?"

The kid swung the backpack to his lap and dangled his feet and looked out at the water.

More cameras came, large ones, with reporters.

"We're live on the City Bridge where a teenager has crawled out to the edge of the bridge."

"He's just been sitting there."

"Has he said anything?"

"Nothing."

"How long has the boy been up there?"

"Ten minutes, maybe."

"Does anyone know who he is?"

No one knew.

"Does anyone know what's in that backpack? Any comment?" the reporter asked the policeman.

The policeman had no comment.

"We'll be standing by for more," said the reporter.

They stood by for an hour. More policemen came and cleared the bridge of pedestrians and bystanders. They brought out a megaphone. "Son, son, SON, SON! You can't just sit there. Would you like assistance, son?"

"Maybe he doesn't speak English," said another policeman.

"He understands we're talking to him. He hasn't turned once."

"Maybe he's, you know, not all there."

"No shit."

"SON! SON!"

"Son, do you like ice cream?"

"What in God's name—"

"Or chicken, maybe? You probably like chicken

better, huh?"

"For God's sake. SON!"

The kid dangled his feet and reached one hand into the bag. He pulled out a mega bottle of Cheezy Balls.

"What's in his hand?"

"Looks like a mega bottle of Cheezy Balls."

"What?"

"Cheezy Balls. I love those things."

"You think he's planning to camp out there?"

"Son, you cannot camp out on the bridge. That is against the law."

"Why don't we go get him?"

"We don't know what he's doing."

"We can't spook him."

"We can't just let him stay there."

"He can't stay there forever."

"He'll have to poop sometime."

"He probably just wants attention."

The kid pulled out a bottled water.

"For God's sake."

"That's a big backpack."

"Captain?"

"Let's send someone out there."

"Send someone out there? What if he jumps?"

"We can't leave him there."

"What about a negotiator?"

"He won't even turn around."

The kid threw a Cheezy Ball down in the water and watch until it was dragged beneath the polluted surface by desperate fish.

"We'll just leave a man here, in case he asks for help or jumps or something. He can't stay there forever."

And the kid couldn't stay there forever. But he could stay for thirty-four hours. In that time, he made the paper. He made the news. His photo was Instagrammed and posted and tweeted.

Strangers discussed him and commented upon him and liked him and disliked him and re-tweeted about him.

It was a crisis; it was a joke; it was a protest; it was madness; it was an anomaly; it was the City. He was some sort of symbol, anyway, though no one agreed on what, exactly, he symbolized.

And then it ended. There was no speech. There was no splash. The kid stood up, dumped out the remainder of his Cheezy Balls in the water, and then threw the bottle down, too.

"Now, that's just awful," said an observer. "That would have been recyclable."

Then the kid carefully walked across the narrow beam, climbed the outside of the chain link fence, swung his leg over—this time just barely snagging his outside pocket and opening a small hole. He lowered himself onto the walkway and was immediately arrested. The cop told him he had the right to remain silent. Anything he said could and would be held against him.

But the kid already knew that.

20

"Thank God, that's over!" said Ms. Eagleton to John Doe, as they folded up their pneumonic device sticky notes and put them in the Idea Jar that Ms. Young was carrying around. John Doe's was blank. Ms. Eagleton's said: *Do All Crazy City Brats Come Crawling Around Are Awful Back Door?*

"This place can really get you down. And I'm a math teacher. There were openings all over the City. Just my luck that I was placed here, you know? I'm applying for a spot at a charter school next year. I've got to get out of here. I don't think I can survive another year."

John Doe had no rejoining comment, which was fine with Ms. Eagleton. She'd been too wrapped up in externalizing her internal monologue, anyway. She was a great soliloquizer, a woman who could be shocked into eloquence by the same old problems every day. And she felt compelled to share her new old discoveries with every person she encountered.

"I can't survive another year! I don't care if I'm up

to my ears in school loan debt," she began. "But it looks like I'm stuck here because—" Ms. Eagleton paused mid-sentence. It looked like she was stuck there because she still couldn't find her one viable ticket out. Over the past two weeks, she'd been searching everywhere for *Tamerlane and Other Poems*. She'd checked the shelves, she'd checked the empty return cart and the check-out desk. She'd even sneaked into Mrs. Brown's office. But the librarian must have hidden the book. That was all there was to it. And Ms. Eagleton, who stood only 5'2", suddenly knew just where it must be.

"Say, sub. Can you see the books on that top shelf?"

John Doe, who was of average height, could, in fact, see onto the top shelf.

"I'm looking for a little book called *Tam*—"

"*Tamerlane and Other Poems*?" said Mrs. Brown, who had materialized behind them.

Ms. Eagleton said, "*Tammy Goes to War*."

"*Tammy Goes to War*?" said Mrs. Brown. "I don't think I've heard of that book before."

"Pity!" said Ms. Eagleton. "Well, then, we'll be off. We have a happy hour to go to."

"A happy hour?" asked John Doe. But the two women were engaged in some sort of a staring contest and didn't hear him. Mrs. Brown narrowed her eyes. Ms. Eagleton narrowed hers. John Doe said, louder, "Are we going to a happy hour?"

"Of course!" said Ms. Eagleton. "We'd better be off." Ms. Eagleton broke eye contact with Mrs. Brown, dug her nails into John Doe's arm, and dragged him through the door. "Come along, sub. I'll introduce you to the pack."

The other teachers had already re-assembled at Benny's in what John Doe would quickly find to be a very sad happy hour. Upon seeing John Doe's fresh face, the teachers quickly circled in.

"Konbanwa," said Mr. White. "How was the first day?"

"What'd you think of the faculty meeting?" asked Mrs. Jackson, who used to teach music but now taught SAT prep.

"Principal Fehler's a real lunatic, huh?" prodded Monsieur Richard. "What?"

John Doe only managed to say that it had been "interesting" before the teachers tore in.

"*Interesting*? You have no idea!" said Monsieur Richard, and then they all started at once, coming from all sides, first with rapid-fire generalities:

"This school system's so incredibly ... "

" ... and then they say it's our fault! *Our* fault? What do they think ... "

" ... on test scores? Have you even seen the questions they put on those ... "

"What do they think we're supposed to do—when these kids come to school without even ... "

"I swear to God, someday I'm going to write a memoir that will absolutely ... "

" ... any brains, you'll get out while you still can!"

Then they started anecdoting over one another:

"Two days ago, there was this huge gang fight in the front hall ... "

" ... a prostitution ring—hand jobs go for five dollars and blow jobs go for ... "

" ... so the kid picks up the trash can and hurls it at the resource officer and tells the office that ... "

"I called his house and just asked for his guardian,

and this man picked up and started cursing, at me, like a fucking … "

" … says he can't vote because he's already a felon! And I say, 'No way, you … "

" … but as it happens it was true: he fathered six kids already—and he's only fourteen! And that's by five different … "

" … none! No parents showed up for parent-teacher conferences, except, of course for Breyona's and Indiana's … "

Somehow—John Doe missed the link—that strand of conversation led to commentary about African American names:

"So then there's Orangejello and Lemonjello—brothers! O-*ran*-jell-o."

" … pronounces it *Brian*, like normal Brian, but it's spelled *B-R-A-I-N* … "

" … named Female but pronounced like Feh-molly, right? Because her mother didn't even …"

" … spelled *L-A-dash*—you know, like a dash, like the punctuation—*A*. Guess how it's pronounced? Ladasha!"

Another round of drinks later, the hilarity delved into depressing speculation:

"If we don't go along with it, you know they'll evaluate us as …"

"It doesn't matter what we do. They're gonna shut us down. I heard from some teachers at … "

" … and no one's perfect, right? Like, if you look at any given teacher you could always find something …"

"… At 302 some inspectors from South Avenue came and pulled the fire alarms and checked all classrooms for word walls …"

" … was penalized because the edges of their curtains didn't line up. They actually took out rulers and … "

" … no takers? Fine. How about 2:1 odds that Howard isn't back for at least two months. That's pretty good odds… "

"Well, there's no way to fight it, is there?"

By this point, John Doe needed some fresh air and finally managed to say so—though he was quite disoriented and had to be led to the exit. The person leading him was a burly man in a gray janitor's jumpsuit that had the name "Bob" embroidered over the City School logo on the right breast pocket.

21

―――――――

"Steady there, Buster!" said Janitor Bob as they pushed through the back door. John Doe took several shallow breaths. Janitor Bob lit a cigarette.

"You smoke?" he asked, holding out his pack of cigarettes.

"Not really," said John Doe.

"Might want to start," he said, lighting his own cigarette. "This here is real tobacco," said Janitor Bob. "Unfiltered. No substitute for the real thing but the real thing. Think about that."

John Doe thought about it.

Janitor Bob said, "I take it that was your first teacher happy hour, Buster?"

"It was."

"Brutal." Janitor Bob stared across the parking lot. John Doe did the same. Bob took a couple puffs of a cigarette and continued. "They don't mean no harm, you know."

"No?" said John Doe.

"They're good people. Poor things. Used to be normal."

"They did?"

"Yessir. Most of them, anyway. I remember many of those teachers' first days. They were excited and nervous and idealistic with full crops of healthy hair—except Monsieur Richard. He's always been a dickhead."

"So what's happened to them?"

Janitor Bob shook his head sadly. "They been reformed. The whole school has."

"Reformed?"

"Yessir. That place has been reformed and re-reformed and un-re-reformed only to be re-re-re-reformed," he said, removing a dirty rag from his belt buckle and wiping his face. "If I had a nickel for every time some suit had come up with the final solution, well." He offered the rag to John Doe, who gestured 'no thanks.' Janitor Bob stuck the rag back in his belt buckle and took another drag from his cigarette. "So much reform has gone on in that school that I think they've forgotten what the thing was originally formed for. And all the while, the ceiling gets leakier, the floor gets dirtier, the shelves get dustier." Janitor Bob shook his head.

"But you know what I say?" Janitor Bob asked.

John Doe didn't.

"The first step to making something better is to stop making it worse."

"What's the second step?"

"What's that?"

"The second step."

"You know, I'd have to think about that. We never made it past the first one." Janitor Bob thought for a moment. "I suppose I could use a bigger broom."

John Doe nodded solemnly and said that he had no idea how bad it was before.

"Well, Buster, not too many on the outside do. They say ignorance is bliss, which is true—but even if you learn something, ignoring works pretty good, too."

Janitor Bob picked something from his teeth and then took another drag.

"So tell me, Buster. How'd you get involved with this group, anyhow?"

John Doe told him.

"Ms. Alloway, again? Seems they really got it in for her."

"Any idea why I might be investigating her?"

Janitor Bob shook his head. "Can't say I do. She always remembered to put her chairs up—and even picked up the big pieces of trash herself. Minds her scraps, you know. The best teachers remember the scraps." Janitor Bob took a final drag from his cigarette, threw the butt on the ground, and stomped it out. "Subs, they always leave a mess. No substitute for the real thing but the real thing—that's what my grandpa always said. Died of diabetes, rest his soul." Janitor Bob bent over and picked up the butt and tossed it in the trashcan. "I'm off, Buster. Best of luck with the investigation. You be careful with that lot, you hear?"

As Janitor Bob walked toward the back gate, something shiny caught his eye. He bent over and picked up a nickel. "Fortune favors the fortunate. That's what I always say," he said. "Only $36.19 to go." Then he left the patio.

John Doe stood outside of Benny's for a moment, working up the courage to go back to the bar to retrieve his jacket. He took a deep breath and entered. He needn't have worried. The place was almost empty. Just after Janitor Bob had helped John Doe out the door, Ms. Young had entered the bar.

"Hey guys!" she'd called out.

And suddenly, the teachers all had somewhere to go. They threw cash on the bar and finished their conversations as they rushed through the front door.

"See you tomorrow!"

"Unless God is merciful!"

"Bye!"

"Goodnight!"

"Seriously, Lexapro! It has worked wonders for me."

"See you in the morning!"

"Wait! Guys! I just got here! Guys!" called out Ms. Young, who was nearly bowled over by the teachers' rapid exit. But the only other soul in Benny's Bar was the bartender, whose name wasn't Benny.

22

"Well, Benny," said Ms. Young, "Just you and me."

The bartender whose name wasn't Benny nodded—his default response as he couldn't understand any English words besides numbers and the names of drinks. Bartenders at Benny's who understood English didn't last that long. The original Benny used to come home so depressed after teacher happy hours that his wife finally gave him an ultimatum: either the teachers went, or she did. Benny tried to get rid of the teachers with crappy specials and offensive jokes, but they had already nested (and rather liked offensive jokes, anyway). His wife left, and that was the last straw for poor Benny. He shot himself in the head, right there in the bar, splattering blood all over the call liquor. Ms. Eagleton had been the first on the scene. It was just her luck. She had come for a Bulleit on the rocks. Typical for Benny to ruin it with a bullet in the head. And the place had been closed for two weeks—during first semester finals, no less.

"You know what's wrong with those teachers?" asked Ms. Young. Most others found Ms. Young insufferable. And, like most insufferable people, she had a good idea why.

"For one, they're jealous. They know I'm special."

The bartender who wasn't named Benny heard "one" and "special" and poured her the drink of the day.

"Also, they're lost. You know? They haven't had their *aha* moment. I've had mine, you know. I remember mine like it was yesterday."

Ms. Young's *aha* moment had occurred last November, during her first and only year of teaching sophomore English. It happened the day that Jazmine Williams smiled. The timing was good because that day Ms. Young was giving her first City Check-up Test.

She knew that Jazmine smiling was a good omen. She could tell that it was going to be her *aha* day. In fact, as she sat in the classroom that day, proctoring the test, she planned her first major television appearance as a spokesperson for inner city teaching success.

"See," she would say, "As a teacher, an inner-city teacher, in a tough, tough inner-city school, you have to learn to recognize small victories."

Oprah would nod, understanding—maybe even reach her hand to Ms. Young. Pat her on the knee. The audience members would lean forward in their seats. Mrs. Young would speak in a charming, animated sort of way—exuding her trademark energy and enthusiasm.

"I mean," she would elaborate, "desert runners, they motivate themselves for long runs—across the desert, no less—by rewarding themselves with a tiny sip of water. Water that they carry in their own mouths, even. They just hold the water in their cheeks until they finish. And then they get that delicious little taste, right at the end. And, well, teachers, we do the same thing. We have to, you know, survive the desert on that little sip of water that we know is coming—especially that first year."

The audience would glow with admiration and appreciation.

Then, proving what a born teacher she was, Ms. Young would turn to the close-up camera: "Also, to my darling students back home," she'd say, smiling, "That—what I just did by comparing teachers to desert runners—that is an analogy." She'd turn back to Oprah and say, "See, once you start teaching, it's just hard to turn it off, you know?"

The audience would laugh warmly.

"Also, do you know how to remember the spelling difference between desert and dessert? There's a simple trick I could teach you all—"

Ms. Young's reverie, though, had been temporarily interrupted by Dontay Peterson.

"No one gives a fuck bout them analogies, Ms. Young," he'd said. Several students laughed. But Jazmine Williams was still smiling, the exact same contented smile.

Ms. Young responded calmly, "Dontay, some people care. You see analogies on TV all the time. We use them when we talk. We have to understand the workings of language to command the power of language." Ms. Young would write that one down later—*command the power of language* was good, and she had come up with it right on the spot. "So go ahead and try on the quiz, okay?"

Dontay had already pulled out his phone, though, to text, sext, Tumbl, tweet, chat, poke, stalk, friend, dash, farm, flick, slash, snap, or message—or to slingshot little birds at pigs. Ms. Young benevolently ig-nored this infraction. To confront it would mean con-fronting the other five students in the room, including Jazmine, who were doing the same thing. And then, to be fair, she'd have to address the two listening to headphones, too. In five months of teaching, Ms. Young knew to choose her battles, see? And small things, well, you can't focus on those, you know?

"That's another thing, Benny," said Ms. Young. "Teachers don't understand what battles to fight, you know?"

Benny didn't know. But Ms. Young didn't know he didn't know. Her thoughts returned back to her *aha* day.

"Okay, class," Ms. Young had said to no one in particular. (No one, in fact.) "Remember, this is very important. This quiz. It's one of those City-wide tests. They look at these scores very seriously. It affects the school and everyone. So, you know, make sure to take this seriously. Also, I wouldn't want to start taking away participation points from people who might be slacking or breaking class rules or anything."

Ms. Young began circling around groups of desks in her classroom, monitoring progress. It's important to be constantly assessing your classroom. Constantly monitoring progress and checking in with the stu-dents. It's the most vital thing in teaching—along with relationship-building, differentiating, and test-prepping.

Jazmine Williams was still smiling. Not a big smile. The corners of her lips were curved just the tiniest bit. A less observant teacher might not even make any-thing of it. But Ms. Young noticed. And then Ms. Young noticed something else. With one hand, so as not to distract any of her classmates, Jazmine was re-moving one of her four-inch golden high heels. She put the heel in an oversized purse under her desk.

Ms. Young tried not to smile as she watched, but undoubtedly her glowing satisfaction escaped through her eyes. She turned away, so as not to distract Jazmine. Jazmine, who was finally starting to get comfortable in her classroom—comfortable enough to take off her shoes. Jazmine Williams finally understood that this classroom could be a safe space for her, that inside her classroom door, she could let go and be herself.

Ms. Young had been paying attention when her Teach For America trainer had advised Ms. Young and her fellow TFA corp members to create a safe space for their students. "You never know what they go though outside your classroom. It's important for them to feel safe. Then you can build a relationship with them. Then, and only then, will you be able to really teach them."

How true, Ms. Young had thought. Those poor little dears. She brought in a nice green couch, painted the room blue, and displayed cheerful houseplants on the window sills.

Still, even with the homey environment, Ms. Young had slightly doubted, in the past five months, her ability to get Jazmine to like her. The other students were easily won over, at least temporarily, with smiles and fist bumps, extra credit packets, permission to charge IPods, permission to curse, candy, pizza, rides home—those kinds of things. Most of her students, Ms. Young believed, really did like her class. And they liked *her*. Even though she was white and, you know, middle-class and privileged and everything, the kids in her classes really liked her—probably more than those arrogant assholes she worked with. It was just a matter of time before those kids started learning. But not Jazmine. For Jazmine, it had always been:

"What the fuck you looking at, dirty-ass bitch?"

"I don't give a shit 'bout your dirty-ass packet."

"I don't need your dirty-ass permission to do nothing."

"I don't want your dirty-ass candy."

"I don't want your dirty-ass pizza."

"You tryin' to kidnap me? I'ma report your dirty-ass."

Ms. Young showered Jazmine with understanding, had pulled her aside to have Fireside Chats, had tried every trick in the *TFA: Managing the Classroom* manual to win her over, but it hadn't worked. Until today.

Jazmine raised her hand. Ms. Young's heart fluttered as she went to her desk and squatted beside it—so as not to disturb the other students in case they decided to pick up their pencils. She noted that Jazmine was now wearing sneakers. This was probably how she dressed when she was safe at home.

"Yes, Jazmine? Do you need some help?"

"Miss, you have a rubber band?"

"A rubber band? Sure."

Ms. Young went back to her desk and rummaged around for a rubber band. Breyona raised her hand.

"Ms. Young?" Breyona called out. "Ms. Young! I need help on my quiz."

"Yeah, just a sec, Breyona. I'll be right there."

Ms. Young finally found a rubber band and brought it to Jazmine.

"Ms. Young! I need some help!" said Breyona.

"Okay, I'll be right there. I'm just helping

Jazmine."

Jazmine inspected the small rubber band. "I mean for hair. A big one."

"Oh. For hair. See, where I'm from, we call rubber bands for hair, 'hair deals.' That's because I'm from kinda a small town in the Midwest—" Ms. Young began, building a relationship.

"MS. YOUNG! What's an analogy?" Breyona called her question across the room.

"Breyona, we talked about this already in class. It's a quiz. I can't tell you now what an analogy is."

Dontay said, "If you not gonna teach us, how we supposed to pass this fucking quiz?"

"I already taught you. Plus, look around, the definition might be somewhere on the wall or something." Ms. Young had definitions for all the terms they covered in class posted over the chips in the cheap blue paint that covered her classroom wall. She had considered covering up the definitions for the quiz, but figured none of the kids would look at them anyway.

Jazmine tugged on her sleeve. "Can I just have yours? I'll trade you for this one."

Ms. Young pulled out her hair band and gave it to Jazmine. She stretched the smaller rubber band around her pony tail and ignored the strands of hair that ripped as she twisted it into place. After all, there were plenty of hairs on her head—and only one Jazmine Williams. That was good, too. Ms. Young was on a roll.

"Class," Ms. Young said, exhilarated at the challenges in front of her, "You know what analogies are. Remember? Remember all the stories I told you that were meant to explain something else?"

"No," said Breyona.

"Well, that's what an analogy is, you know? A story about something familiar that explains something unfamiliar."

"Oh! Like that running thing you told us," Dontay said.

"Yes!" Ms. Young was excited. "Exactly! Fantastic! Dontay, you are so smart when you apply yourself."

"Fuck yeah. You all hear that? I'm smart as shit!" Dontay paused for a moment. "What was that running thing again?"

"You dumb as shit," another student chimed in.

"No, no. No one's dumb. The running thing was this: Desert runners run miles across the desert, and their only reward is just a little taste of water every so often. That's just like being a student. You know? You work really, really hard, and your little reward is a good grade on your report card."

"Yeah, not something good, like money."

"Right! Good! So desert runners are to water as students are to..."

"Money!"

"Not money. Think about it."

"Grades!"

"YES!"

"I'ma kill this quiz." Dontay said, proceeding to answer the next five questions incorrectly. The rest of the class followed suit. Ms. Young, again, circled around, beaming at the effort.

Jazmine had her long weave pulled into as tight a bun as she could. It wasn't her usual look, but she was probably just trying to get it off her neck as she focused on her quiz. Jazmine noticed Ms. Young looking at her. She graciously put her phone in her lap and fake-read her quiz. It was the nicest response Ms. Young had ever gotten from her. Ms. Young continued to watch as Jazmine, with one hand, subtly removed a long, dangling earring.

Dontay, sitting across from her, looked up. "Oh, shi-it," he said.

"What's the problem?" asked Ms. Young, ready to defend Jazmine's right to comfort over style—or to help him with a word on the quiz.

"Nothing," Dontay said, looking back at his quiz and circling another wrong answer.

Ms. Young smiled to herself and went back to her desk. She typed, *We have to understand the workings of language to command the power of language.* Then she typed, *There were plenty of hairs on her head, but only one Jazmine Williams.* She wanted to remember everything about this day perfectly. This was probably the turning point day. Like when Michelle Pfeiffer runs around the track a bunch of times. Or when Hilary Swank does the thing with the line, and her students start to trust her. This was it. This was what teaching for America was all about.

Jazmine Williams looked up from her lap, where she was texting on her phone, reasonably discreetly. She met Ms. Young's eyes and seemed to look through them, straight through the back of her head. Jazmine brought her phone to her desk and pushed a green button. She looked up again and smiled, this time with a little more curve. She leaned over, whispered something to Dontay, and handed him her purse.

The door to another classroom slammed loudly. Ms. Young walked toward the classroom door, calmly, to investigate. Just as she got to her door, an angry face popped up in the door's dirty window, an angry finger pointed straight through Ms. Young to Jazmine. "I'MA FUCK THAT BITCH UP!"

"I'MA SHUT YOUR DIRTY-ASS MOUTH!" Jazmine flew past Mrs. Young, flung the door open, and ran into the hallway.

Dontay yelled, "FIGHT!" The class, on cue, rushed after Jazmine. Quizzes, pencils, and chairs flew around the room. The dried-up houseplant on the sill nearest the door crashed to the floor.

Stunned, Ms. Young staggered to the calming green couch, ignoring the Dorito crumbs that were smashed into the cushion. She picked up a test that had floated across the room and was resting, facedown, directly in front of her.

She barely registered Ms. Fehler call for "SCHOOL POLICE! SCHOOL POLICE ON THE SECOND FLOOR!" over the intercom. She didn't hear Dontay yell, "MACE!"

But almost as suddenly as they had disappeared, the students were back at their seats. Dontay slammed the door shut. They picked up the nearest quiz or book or pencil and faked studentry until the commotion in the hallway stopped.

"We still have to finish this fucking test?" Dontay asked, turning to address Ms. Young, who was still in bewilderment on the couch, still clutching the test booklet. And then she had her 'aha' moment:

If something unforeseeable happened to a desert runner—say, he tripped over a little cactus sprig or got beaten by a gang of desert bandits—if something like that happened, and he swallowed his mouth water, no one would blame him for accepting another swig from a generous Samaritan passerby, right? And these poor kids. Ms. Young looked around her classroom at the flushed faces of her students, minus Jazmine—their eyes watering from the mace that the school police used to break up the girls. Mace! These poor kids. Bless their little blood-shot eyes and blackened lungs. They never catch a break. They need a Samaritan. They all needed a win. If only she could do something. And then she realized she could.

"You all have been through a lot today. I understand. Teachers, we can understand things like that. If you need a desert drink, I'll can be your Samaritan. You know what I mean?"

They didn't. She tried again.

"What I'm saying is we can't lose sight of the ultimate goals of education—which is to help shape young minds. And part of that is teaching that mercy can sometimes be a sign of strength, you know?"

They didn't.

"What I mean is, I'll give you the answers to all the even problems. You worry about the odds."

"Ah!" said Dontay.

"Aha, you mean!" corrected Ms. Young. Then she began calling out the even answers. That went so well, that she threw in a few of the odds. "Erase completely, darlings!" she'd instructed. It had been the right thing to do.

"You see, Benny," Ms. Young went on, sipping on the special. "I've always had so much to give to this world, you know? Even if my high school classmates, my high school students, or my fellow high school teachers don't realize it yet. I'm a born educator. I'll make my mark on this world, you know?"

The bartender who wasn't Benny didn't know.

"So I decided to forego my second year of teaching in favor of, you know, capitalizing on my strengths—so I can affect greater change on the country's education policy," continued Ms. Young. "What's so wrong with that?"

The bartender who wasn't Benny shrugged.

"I just think that other teachers out there are getting insufficient training, and I really believe that I can help. You know, I just learned so much that year. And, I mean, my test scores, they went up so much! My pass rate was three times as high as my department's average. So, you know."

On hearing the word "three," the bartender who wasn't Benny shook his head. No way this lady needed three more.

"What? You don't believe me, either? Research clearly says teachers are the biggest factor in a student's success." Ms. Young said, "See, teachers are really struggling—and it's not because they're incompetent or lazy. They need help on a systematic level. We need to train them. Then we need to hold them accountable," Ms. Young paused and looked the bartender who wasn't Benny meaningfully, but, of course, he didn't catch the meaning. "Teachers. Accountability. That's the direction of education. That's what American education is all about," she said. "That and charter schools."

Ms. Young finished the speech, which had been the same speech that had landed her the UCAN edUCAtioN job. It sounded just as good this time. "Smart as shit," as good ole Dontay would say. Ms. Young might have wondered whatever happened to good ole Dontay, but at that exact moment, John Doe walked back into the bar.

23

Ms. Young looked up from her drink special and saw John Doe. "Oh! You!" She nearly skipped over to John Doe.

"Me?" said John Doe.

"You're the one I was looking for. Principal—" Ms. Young paused and looked around cautiously, even though the only other soul in the bar was the bartender who wasn't named Benny. She lowered her voice. "Principal Fehler sent me to get you."

"Why'd she send you?"

"Principal Fehler doesn't fraternize with the help."

"Is this about the mole thing again?"

Ms. Young shhhed him. "Yes," she whispered. "I'll take you to her office."

When they arrived, Principal Fehler told Ms. Young that she could go back to her sticky notes—and to shut the door behind her. Ms. Young said that she had already gone through the sticky notes and that *Dog Ate Cat Chips Because Cat Chips Are Almost Always Better, Duh!* was the clear winner. Principal Fehler said it was important enough to warrant a second look. Ms. Young, who wanted to be important almost as much as she wanted to be famous and well-liked, beamed.

"Close the door behind you!"

Ms. Young did so, and Principal Fehler turned to John Doe.

"Well?" she said.

"No one said anything about it," said John Doe. "I don't think anyone really cares, to be honest."

Principal Fehler rubbed her chin. "Is that true?"

"Yes," said John Doe.

"I understand that you had a prolonged conversation with Janitor Bob."

"How did you know that?"

"I have moles everywhere."

"I know that!" John Doe was becoming disgusted with that conversation.

Ms. Young popped open the door. "Guess what? Mr. White's was all in Japanese! You want to hear it?"

"Of course not," said Principal Fehler. John Doe also shook his head. Ms. Young frowned.

"Should I close the door, then?"

Principal Fehler glared at her. Ms. Young closed the door gently. Principal Fehler turned her attention back to John Doe.

"What was it, exactly, that you and Bob had to say to one another?"

"I was just asking him about Ms. Alloway."

"*Ms. Alloway!*"

"Ms. Alloway."

"What does that horrible teacher have to do with anything? She's taken care of."

"Why is she horrible?"

"*Why is she horrible!*"

"Why is she horrible?"

"You have no idea!"

"I have no idea."

"You don't know!"

"I don't know."

"Let me show you something!" said Principal Fehler, turning toward her filing cabinet. She yanked out a green folder labeled *Alloway, Ellen*. She opened it and showed John Doe a handwritten petition. "Do you know what this is?" she asked.

"Looks like a petition for better school food," said John Doe. "Kimi got an A- on it."

"And this one?" said Principal Fehler, flipping to the next sheet.

"A petition to count pizza sauce as a vegetable and stop serving spinach. Looks like Ms. Alloway didn't like that one too much."

"And this?"

"A petition for you to resign." John Doe whistled. "Lots of signatures on that one."

"And this one?" she said.

"A petition to stop taking the exams in May."

"Exactly. And there are dozens more."

"Exams?"

"Petitions," she paused. "And exams, for that matter. But the petitions are the point. Don't you see? Ms. Alloway was trying to incite a riot; she was trying to undermine my authority; she was trying to sabotage this school!"

"Oh," said John Doe. "That's why she's on leave?"

"No," said Principal Fehler, "That's why she was on leave the *second* time—last year. Unfortunately, as it turned out, her students' test scores were still as good as the students for all the other teachers in the school. So the Achievement and Accountability Department told me that that the petitions were not sufficient grounds for a leave of absence." Principal Fehler put the petitions back in the folder and replaced it in the filing cabinet. "And they actually liked the pizza as a vegetable idea. Apparently it's cheaper than spinach."

"So why is she on leave this time?"

"That's what I've been trying to figure out," said Principal Fehler.

"That's what *I've* been trying to figure out!" said John Doe.

"I couldn't get her to admit to a thing," said Principal Fehler.

"Does she have a thing to admit?"

"Everyone has a thing! She'll come clean."

"What if she is already clean?"

"She's not clean! No one's clean. Everyone's got dirt."

"Even you?"

Principal Fehler frowned. "Of course not. What have you heard?"

"I haven't heard anything! That's the problem."

"That's not a problem. I mind my p's and q's."

"But Ms. Alloway doesn't."

"No, she does, too. That's the problem. That woman documents everything!" Principal Fehler slammed her hand on the desk."

"So *that's* the problem?" asked John Doe.

"Of course it's the problem."

"And *that's* why she's on leave."

"Of course not. You can't put someone on leave for documenting!"

"So what is the issue then?

"That's what I'm trying to find out!" yelled Principal Fehler. She had finally decided that John Doe was, in fact, playing against her. John Doe decided that he didn't like her overbearing tone. It reminded him of his mother.

"So there's nothing further to investigate?"

"We can't be sure until the investigation is complete," said Principal Fehler, who went to the refrigerator and retrieved some leftover pea soup. She began to slurp it down, to John Doe's disgust.

"But how will we know when it's done?"

"We won't. We won't know. But as long as Ms. Alloway is out, we can continue with Test Prep Analytics. After all, it's all about the—"

"Kids?"

"Exactly! It's all about the kids' test scores."

"But don't you think—"

Ms. Young knocked on the door and opened it at the same time. "I've got it!" she said. "*Daring And Creative Children Become Completely Cool Adults And Accomplish Big Deeds.* What do you think?"

"I like the cat chips one better," said Principal Fehler.

John Doe disagreed.

"So?" said Principal Fehler. "Who asked you?"

"Ms. Young."

"Ms. Young, did you ask him?"

"I said you," she said. "It was ambiguous."

"Did you say me or was it ambiguous? Make up your mind."

"I said you," said Ms. Young.

"There you have it!" said Principal Fehler. "Ms. Young, please see this gentleman out of the school. We will not be in need of your services anymore, sir."

24

Processing. Please Wait. Processing. Please Wait. Processing. John Doe stared at the comforting words as they flashed on his computer. He was glad to be back in the Department of Human Capital that morning. *Upload complete. Ready!*

"Carol!" said John Doe. "I'm ready for the next folder."

Carol waddled in, removed the next folder from the file cabinet, and handed it to him. John Doe licked his fingers and grabbed the top paper. He placed it on the scanner. He hit the *SCAN NOW* button. Carol watched in awe of his technology skills.

"I'm sure glad you kids know how to work technology," said Carol. "Heaven knows, if you had been out another day, I'd have had to do it." They both watched the screen. "I'd have messed everything up."

Processing. Please Wait. Processing. Please Wait. Processing. Please Wait. Upload Complete. Ready

Carol shook her head again in wonder. "Look there, it's right on the screen!" John Doe dragged the document to the *IN* folder. Carol whistled. "Would you look at that?" she asked.

John Doe pushed back his shoulders, proudly.

Carol removed the sheet of paper from the scanner and added the next one. John Doe pushed the button.

Processing. Please Wait.

"I could watch this all day," said Carol.

"I can teach you how to work it," said John Doe.

"Oh, no! I'd just mess it up. I like to watch, though. It's a shame I have other things to do today. Did you know we have thirteen more long-term sub requests for the district today? That's the largest number since the Swine Flu epidemic."

Processing. Please Wait.

"No substitute for the real thing but the real thing," said John Doe.

"Carol!" said Manager Manly from his office. "Carol! Get in here!"

Carol went into the office. John Doe idly eavesdropped from the scanner.

"Carol! What in God's name is this guy doing here?"

Manager Manly nodded toward Creepy McGoo, who was lurking in the corner of Manager Manly's office.

Carol shivered. "I don't know! Did you ask him?"

"No! I'm asking you."

"Sir," said Carol. "Why are you here?"

"The Room's full," said Creepy McGoo. "So L'Blanc told me to make myself useful somewhere else." He tried to smile winningly, but the effect was frightful.

"Carol!" said Manager Manly. "Get rid of him!"

"Did you try the Department of Achievement and Accountability?"

"They said to never come back."

"Well, you can't come here, either. Check out Student Support and Safety."

"No one was there."

"Well, you can't stay here."

Creepy McGoo stayed there.

"Shoo!" said Carol. "Shoo! You go on back to the Room. I'm sure she can squeeze you in. Shoo! Tell her she can send down that Wallflower Girl again, if she needs to."

Wallflower Girl, whom no one had noticed sitting on a chair in the corner, cleared her throat and waved.

"My God!" said Manager Manly. "These teachers are really getting out of hand. South Avenue is completely infested!"

"Teachers, teachers everywhere, and not a spot to teach," said Wallflower Girl, finally finding something profound enough to break her silence. She stood up proudly and prepared to say a few more things that she'd had on her mind.

"Get her out of here, too!" said Manager Manly.

Carol looked at Manager Manly. Wallflower Girl looked at Manager Manly. Creepy McGoo looked at Manager Manly. Manager Manly looked at some papers on his desk, squinted, counted to ten and then looked up again. They were all still looking at him.

"Carol!"

"Shoo!" said Carol to Creepy McGoo and the Wallflower Girl. "Get out! Shoo!" She herded them as far as the front desk. Then Carol tottered to the back office. John Doe looked up, met Creepy McGoo's eyes, and looked back down.

Processing. Please Wait.

"I hate this place," said the Wallflower Girl.

"Can't get better 'til we stop making it worse," said John Doe, without looking up.

"What does that mean? How don't we make it worse?"

John Doe shrugged.

Processing. Please Wait.

25

Erica Meddler had some very specific ideas about how not to make it worse, though. And that morning in track practice, she had acted on them. She had shown up with a dab of dark makeup under her eyes, slumping shoulders, and a slight limp.

"Meddler!" Monsieur Richard said at the start of practice. "Meddler, how about a race?"

Erica protested. "No thanks, Coach," she said. "I'm not feeling good."

"What? You're on the track team but afraid to race? You too scared to race an old man like me? You think you can't take a thirty-three-year-old? Fifty pushups says I can take you."

"I'm just tired. I'll race you tomorrow."

"Maybe if you ran the halls a little less, you wouldn't be so tired."

"Coach!"

"If you can't run with the big dogs, stay on the porch," said Monsieur Richard, reading from his coaching T-shirt.

Erica shrugged.

"You think you're getting a scholarship, acting like

a wussy? Man up!"

Gerald Baker, who was glad that Monsieur Richard had singled out Erica instead of him, echoed his taunt.

Janae Watkins, a chubby shot-putter who had a crush on Gerald, expressed her feelings for him by telling him to "Shut the fuck up."

Breyona Phillips asked if they could just start stretching.

But Monsieur Richard ignored them all. "Coach!" Monsieur Richard mimicked in a voice that sounded nothing like Erica's. "Coach! I'm too tired, Coach."

Gerald forced a laugh, even though he didn't think it was funny; Janae forced a frown, even as her heart fluttered; the other athletes forced themselves to look down, except Breyona—who had never learned to disguise her feelings.

"Coach, please? Can we warm up?" Breyona asked.

Monsieur Richard finally turned his attention to her and was about to invite her to participate, but Erica cut him off.

"Fine," said Erica. "I'll do it."

"Oh yeah? Now you think you're all tough?"

"Let's just get this over with," she said.

"Now you think you're a big dog, huh?"

They lined up at the starting line. He instructed Gerald to count them down. "Go," Gerald said. But Monsieur Richard held up his hand.

"That's not how you start a race, retard."

Gerald shrugged. "You say on your mark, get set, go!"

"On your mark, get set, go."

Monsieur Richard and Erica took off. Monsieur

Richard jumped to a ten-yard lead, then he slowed to let Erica catch him. But Erica slowed down, too. So Monsieur Richard slowed even more. When she finally made it within a step, he sprinted off ten more yards. She slowed down even more. He slowed down to let her almost catch him. And on they went in the same pattern. It wasn't nearly as fun for Monsieur Richard as usual, but at least it would teach Erica a lesson.

On the last stretch, he slowed down, as usual, so that she could actually draw even with him. Then Monsieur Richard took off toward the finish line. But Erica took off, too. She sprinted out five yards ahead of him. He used every ounce of strength he had to close the gap. Sweat flowed from his pores. But fifty yards from the end, she re-opened the gap and sprinted to the finish line, several yards ahead of him.

In fact, technically, Monsieur Richard never finished. A couple of yards before the end, Monsieur Richard's muscles clenched, he felt light-headed, and then he went limp on the track.

Erica calmly gathered her belongings, said "deuces," and went inside to shower. The other athletes stood silently, near the finish line—keeping their distance in case he suddenly perked up. But he couldn't arouse himself. Finally, Breyona went to the main office to get some help.

26

Ms. Noreen told Breyona that whatever she had to say could wait—couldn't she see that Mr. Howard was talking? It was rude to interrupt. Breyona apologized. Ms. Noreen went back to ignoring Mr. Howard.

Mr. Howard said, "I have to take care of me, you know? So here it is."

He thrust a piece of paper between Ms. Noreen's eyes and her book.

"What's this?" asked Ms. Noreen, brushing it to the side.

"It's my resignation."

"No, it's not," said Ms. Noreen, brushing it to the side.

"What do you mean, it's not?" asked Mr. Howard.

"I mean that's not the form for resigning," said Ms. Noreen.

"I stayed up all night writing this!" said Mr. Howard. "I, I poured my heart and soul into it. It's a good letter!"

And it was a good letter. In it was insightful commentary on the structural problems of the City School District, touching stories of students that he had interacted with but felt unable to truly help, and an honest account of the internal turmoil that he had gone through—the guilt, the rationalization, the compromising—before finally deciding that he would go work in insurance with his uncle, also a former teacher. He didn't feel the school system provided the level of support necessary for teachers to succeed; he didn't want to be part of such a broken and, at times, corrupt institution; he felt that schools were used as political tools to take the public's attention away from larger societal issues related to poverty; and he could make more money selling insurance, anyway. It was a good letter, and Mr. Howard had looked forward to the moment of presenting it all evening.

"It's not official," said Ms. Noreen. "No one will even look at that."

"But—"

Ms. Noreen opened one of her desk drawers and retrieved form *4.2.1B City School Resignation*. She held it up. "This is what you need to fill out. Just put in the date of resignation and sign it."

"That's it?"

"Could have saved you some time last night."

"But I have things to say."

"There's a questionnaire that you can complete. You can make your comments there." She showed him the back of the form. There were three multiple-choice questions—each with the same answer possibilities of *extremely satisfied, somewhat satisfied, somewhat dissatisfied, and very dissatisfied*.

Mr. Howard read the questions. *"How satisfied were you with your students? How satisfied were you with you principal, fellow staff, and school? How satisfied were you with your own performance?"* Mr. Howard sniffed back the mucus that was pushing out of the front of his face. "How am I supposed to answer those questions?"

"For God's sake, Mr. Howard. It's multiple-choice. They made it easy on you."

"But—"

"Mr. Howard, there are other people in this office who need attention, too, you know," said Ms. Noreen, withdrawing the paper from his grasp.

They both glanced over to Breyona. She rocked from one foot to the other, reading a poster that said: *For success, attitude is as important as ability.* It had a picture of an ant moving a big stick.

"Why are you here, again?" Ms. Noreen asked her. But before Breyona could answer, the door swung open and Mrs. Brown came in with two boxes, one stacked precariously on top of the other.

"Oh, good. Mr. Howard. Help me with these, will you?" She had thrust the two boxes into his hands before she finished the sentence. He stumbled backwards a little. "And Breyona, great! There are two more packed boxes by the library door. Can I trust you to get those and bring them straight here without distributing them?"

Breyona nodded.

"OK, then. Scoot."

Breyona scooted.

"Where do these go?" asked Mr. Howard.

"Storage closet. Noreen, could I have the key?" Noreen handed Mrs. Brown the ring, which must have had twenty keys on it. Mrs. Brown tried several while Mr. Howard sweated under the strain and Ms. Noreen shook her head.

"Why are we putting these boxes in the storage closet?" asked Mr. Howard.

"Mind your own business," said Mrs. Brown, eyeing him. Mrs. Brown wasn't going to take any chances. Ever again. Not after catching Ms. Eagleton snooping around again after the faculty meeting. She had spent the rest of the night organizing all the books into three groups: books that had been checked out, books that might conceivably be checked out, and books that no one had any interest in. Any books that had been checked out before—your *Harry Potters*, your *Hunger Games*, your romances, your books on required or recommended reading lists, and Oprah's Book Club titles—were boxed up. Mrs. Brown planned to lock them in various places throughout the school, for safekeeping. Books that Mrs. Brown thought might be checked out—anything under three hundred pages with a picture on the cover—she moved behind the desk. The other books—three copies of *Don Quixote*, twenty-six dictionaries, a set of 1982 encyclopedias, two thesauruses, and the entire Russian Literature section (except for a certain edition of *Anna Karenina* that had a seductive woman on the cover) were left on the shelves as non-circulating reference materials. "Just put them on the back shelf. There should be an old poetry book back there already."

Mr. Howard didn't see the book. "I don't see a—"

"OK!" said City Teacher Union Representative Aliyah Deere, SCS, SC, BHCO, JSC, NHSFA, FLCF, as she burst through the door tailed by her seven students—six carrying order sheets and one with a moneybag. "We've got cookie dough for National Honor Society, Bon Bons for Foreign Language Club, candy bars for Black History Club, frozen pizzas for Student Council, and, uh --"

"Magazines for swim team," said the Magazine

Kid.

"Right! Magazines for swim team and also raffle tickets for the debate team." City Teacher Union Representative Aliyah Deere, SCS, SC, BHCO, JSC, NHSFA, FLCF, was also the debate coach (DC). "What can I put you down for?"

City Teacher Union Representative Aliyah Deere, SCS, SC, BHCO, JSC, NHSFA, FLCF, DC, and the seven students looked around. Mrs. Brown pointed to the space in the closet where Mr. Howard should set the boxes. Mr. Howard grunted. Ms. Noreen asked if they had Butterfinger.

"Ran out," said Candy Bar kid.

"Nothing then," said Ms. Noreen.

"Mr. Howard?" asked City Teacher Union Representative Aliyah Deere, SCS, SC, BHCO, JSC, NHSFA, FLCF, DC. He set the books on the shelf.

"Uh, one of each, I guess?"

The seven students worked out the type of cookie dough, flavor of Bon Bons, brand of candy bar, topping of pizza, title of magazine and number of raffle tickets—"One? Really? We're selling 6 for $5."

While they were talking, City Teacher Union Representative Aliyah Deere, SCS, SC, BHCO, JSC, NHSFA, FLCF, DC, began straightening various papers in the office. She came across Mr. Howard's letter, which Ms. Noreen had allowed to fall to the floor.

"What's this?" she asked, holding up the letter.

Breyona bumbled in with the box. "Where do I put this?" she asked.

"You left a box there?" asked Mrs. Brown. "What if someone takes it?"

"It was too heavy," said Breyona. "What's in there anyway?"

"Books, of course!"

"Oh," said Breyona.

"Well, go get the other one."

"BRB," said Breyona.

"Thanks, Mr. Howard," said the Money Bag Kid. "We need separate checks for the pizza, cookie dough, and magazines and cash for the Bon Bons, candy bars, and raffle tickets."

Mr. Howard pulled out his wallet and checkbook.

"You got Snickers?" Ms. Noreen asked the Candy Bar Kid.

"Yeah," said the student.

"Regular or almond."

"Both," said the kid.

"This is a good letter," said City Teacher Union Representative Aliyah, SCS, SC, BHCO, JSC, NHSFA, FLCF, DC.

"Nothing then," said Ms. Noreen. Ms. Noreen turned to the Bon Bon kid. "What are these?" she asked.

"Bon Bons," said the Bon Bon kid.

Ms. Noreen pulled out a package and examined the nutrition facts on the back. Then she scrunched her nose and put them back.

Breyona came back with the other box of books.

"Just set them down on the floor," said Mrs. Brown. "And wait right there while I count them." Mrs. Brown squatted down on the floor and began counting the books.

Mr. White almost tripped over her as he came in with a seven-page worksheet packet to be copied front-to-back and stapled. "Sorry about that, Mrs. Brown!" said Mr. White. "Or, as they say in Japan, Sōrī."

The Bon Bon kid, Cookie Dough Kid, and Raffle Kid suddenly got giggly. "Want some candy?" the Bon Bon kid asked, fluttering her eyes.

"Just leave the copies with me," said Ms. Noreen, fluttering her eyes. "I'll take care of them first thing and bring them to you."

"Arigatō," said Mr. White to Ms. Noreen. Then he turned to the Bon Bon kid. He reached into his tight back pocket and removed a Japanese candy wrapper. "This is what they eat in Japan," he explained. Then he patted the Bon Bon kid on the head and held the door open for Ms. Young, who was also coming in with a paper of her own.

"Thanks, Mr. White!" said Ms. Young, fluttering her eyes. Her paper was a T-shirt order form to collect sizing information for T-shirts that would be distributed on the day of the State Exams. The front of the T-shirts had a picture of a dog eating a bag of chips that had a picture of a cat on them. The back, in clear, easy to read lettering—with the first letter of each word in boldface—said **D**og **A**te **C**at **C**hips **B**ecause **C**at **C**hips **A**re **A**lmost **A**lways **B**etter, **D**uh!

He smiled and looked at the picture. "Those look like Japanese chips," he said. Then he strolled out. All of the women in the office watched him go.

"I need copies!" said Ms. Young to Ms. Noreen.

"About that form," said Mr. Howard.

"What'd you say that raffle was for?" Ms. Noreen asked the Raffle Kid.

"I need some copies!" said Ms. Young. "It's urgent school business."

"An X-Box," said the Raffle Kid.

"Just let me have the form, and I'll go," said Mr. Howard.

"What form?" asked Mrs. Brown.

"White people snoopy," said the Raffle Kid.

"I'm resigning," said Mr. Howard, preparing to defend his decision against any arguments from Mrs. Brown.

"Oh," said Mrs. Brown. "Makes sense."

"Good for you!" said Ms. Young.

"Good for whom?" asked Dr. Luney, who was navigating through the sea of people in the office. "My, my! What a little party we're having here!"

"Mr. Howard's quitting," explained Mrs. Brown.

"Congratulations, sir," said Dr. Luney, shaking his hand a little too hard.

"But they won't accept my resignation letter," said Mr. Howard.

"Well, I'm sure you can work that out with Ms. Noreen," said Dr. Luney, releasing Mr. Howard's hand and slipping into his private office. "Let me know if you need—" he began, but cut himself off by slamming the door.

"Copies!" said Ms. Young.

"The form?" asked Mr. Howard.

"An X-Box?" asked Ms. Noreen, shaking her head at the raffle kid. "What would I do with an X-Box?"

"ATTENTION STUDENTS AND TEACHERS IN THE MAIN OFFICE!" said Principal Fehler's voice over the intercom. They could hear the same voice, a half second ahead of the overhead speaker voice coming from behind the Principal's closed office door. "UNLESS YOU HAVE URGENT BUSINESS IN THE MAIN OFFICE, PLEASE LEAVE. I RE-PEAT. UNLESS YOU HAVE URGENT BUSI-NESS IN THE OFFICE, PLEASE LEAVE."

There was a pause. Everyone stopped talking, but

no one left.

"MS. NOREEN?"

Ms. Noreen rolled her eyes. "I'm only one person," she said.

"EVERYBODY LEAVE!" commanded the almost simultaneous voices. Instead, a very tan Ms. Morose entered.

"Well," she said. "I'm back."

"Did you find Juan Alamarez?" asked Ms. Eagleton, who had followed her in. On seeing Ms. Eagleton, Mrs. Brown quickly slammed the storage closet door. Luckily for her, the kids had already swarmed Ms. Eagleton, hawking their goods.

"Yes," said Ms. Morose. "But he wouldn't sign the papers." In fact, Juan had stumbled upon Ms. Morose as she was drinking a strawberry margarita, poolside. He had just gotten a job as a poolside server. Ms. Morose had asked him to sign the papers, to transfer to 406, but Juan had refused.

"That school worse than 405," he'd said.

"Yes, but you aren't actually attending it," said Ms. Morose. "You're in Mexico."

"Right, but I heard things. If I'm not attending a school, I'd rather not attend 405 than 406. They beat up Hispanics in 406." Juan had paused. "Can you get me into Martin High? Or King High?" he'd asked.

"They're full," she said.

"Luther?" he asked.

"Also full. Plus, with your attendance record, they aren't likely to let you into a Charter anyway."

"Well, maybe if I were in a decent school, I'd show up."

"You're in Mexico."

"No thanks to Luther High!"

157

"So you won't sign?" she asked.

Juan shook his head. "I heard they basically give away diplomas at 406. I don't want no diploma from there. Better to be a dropout than have a diploma from 406!"

And so Ms. Morose had returned, empty-handed. "There's not a chance in hell Luther will let him in," she explained to Ms. Eagleton. "I'm sorry. I tried."

"TEACHERS AND STUDENTS AND COUN-SELORS," began the almost simultaneous voices from the overhead speaker and behind the principal's door. "PLEASE RETURN TO YOUR CLASS-ROOMS—"

But at that moment, Jazmine Williams swung open the door. "Hey!" she said. No one turned. "HEY!" she yelled, loudly enough that Principal Fehler could hear her through the door and stopped mid-announcement

"What?" said Ms. Noreen.

"Thought you should know that Monsieur Richard is being taken to the hospital. You not hear the sirens?"

Every head shook.

"Jesus Christ," said Jazmine. "What's wrong with you people?"

"What's wrong with Monsieur Richard?" asked City Teacher Union Representative Aliyah Deere, SCS, SC, BHCO, JSC, NHSFA, FLCF, DC.

"He a dickhead," offered the Bon Bon kid.

"Heat stroke or something," said Jazmine.

"Is he dead?" Mr. Howard asked in a trembling voice.

"No," said Jazmine. "They got him up. But he went to the hospital as a precaution."

The teachers processed this a moment.

"Copies!" said Ms. Young.

"Can you believe that?" said Ms. Eagleton. "Heat stroke! I should have thought of that. Bet he gets short term disability and workman's comp!"

"Can you just give me the form?" asked Mr. Howard.

"You know you have to take your resignation to South Avenue anyway," said Ms. Noreen, finally handing him the form. "I'm certainly not taking it for you."

"I'll take it for you," offered City Teacher Union Representative Aliyah Deere, SCS, SC, BHCO, JSC, NHSFA, FLCF, DC, who had just finished reading Mr. Howard's letter. "I'm headed up there myself." She paused. "Can you really make more money selling insurance?"

"Bon Bons?" the Bon Bon kid asked Ms. Morose.

"PLEASE RETURN TO YOUR—" began Principal Fehler.

But as she said it, Antonio popped his head in the door. "Tres, dos, uno!" he said. The bell rang, cutting off Principal Fehler.

"He always be doin' that," said Breyona to no one in particular. "Freaks me out."

The teachers and students quickly finished their business: Ms. Noreen gave Mr. Howard the form and started the copies for Mr. White (Ms. Young could wait); Mrs. Brown locked the cabinet; the students wrote down final orders. Within thirty seconds, every teacher, student, and administrator had dispersed, muttering about how there's never enough time in the morning to get anything done.

27

After collecting all the forms from School 405 that were to be delivered to South Avenue, City Teacher Union Representative Aliyah Deere, SCS, SC, BHCO, JSC, NHSFA, FLCF, DC, packed her seven students, the six order sheets, and one moneybag into the car and drove to the City School Headquarters.

She also had five forms with her, including her own resignation form. Mr. Howard's letter had caused City Teacher Union Representative Aliyah Deere, SCS, SC, BHCO, JSC, NHSFA, FLCF, DC, to take pause. And taking pause is one thing that over-extended teachers should never do. Taking pause forces them to reassess their lives, to admit that, per-haps, they had been beating their heads against the same old walls for long enough. It was time to move on to new walls. New walls in a new office with a new set of letters to follow her name.

City Teacher Union Representative Aliyah Deere, SCS, SC, BHCO, JSC, NHSFA, FLCF, DC, would become Lead Underwriter Aliyah Deere, Associate in Insurance Services (AIS), Certified Insurance Counse-lor (CIC), Associate in Risk Management (ARM),

Chartered Property Casualty Underwriter (CPCU), Personal Lines Coverage Specialist (PLCS), Chartered Life Underwriter (CLU), and Certified Risk Manager (CRM). Sure, future Lead Underwriter Aliyah Deere, AIS, CIC, ARM, CPCU, PLCS, CLU, CRM, would miss teaching. She'd miss her students, too, though all but Money Bags were graduating anyway. And Money Bags was really a brown-nosing, résumé-obsessed asshole. Plus, she rationalized, she could always be a classroom volunteer (CV).

Future Lead Underwriter Aliyah Deere, AIS, CIC, ARM, CPCU, PLCS, CLU, CRM, CV, parked her car in the handicapped spot near the entrance of the City School Headquarters and prepared for one last battle.

The troops marched into the Office of Human Capital, prepared with papers, pitches and pleas. "Excuse me!" said Future Lead Underwriter Aliyah Deere, AIS, CIC, ARM, CPCU, PLCS, CLU, CRM, CV—loudly enough to be heard through the closed inner office door of Manager Manly, who quietly crept to the door and turned the lock. She dinged the bell three times. "Excuse me!" John Doe, who was processing and waiting at the scanner station continued processing. "Excuse me!" she said, dinging two more times. "I have some things to discuss with you! I can see you, you know!"

At just that moment, Creepy McGoo, who had been hiding under the front desk, popped up.

"Yes?" he asked, giving a friendly smile that froze the children in fear. "Can I help you?"

Future Lead Underwriter Aliyah Deere, AIS, CIC, ARM, CPCU, PLCS, CLU, CRM, CV, cringed. "I'm just dropping these off," she said quickly. She dropped the forms on the desk.

"Is that candy?" asked Creepy McGoo, pointing to the Bon Bon Kid.

Future Lead Underwriter Aliyah Deere, AIS, CIC, ARM, CPCU, PLCS, CLU, CRM, CV, directed her little soldiers to retreat. "Hurry along! HUSTLE!" She slammed the door behind her. "Don't sell candy to strangers!" she instructed as she led them out the door.

Creepy McGoo gathered the forms and brought them to Manager Manly's office. He knocked.

"Not occupied," said Manager Manly.

"She's gone," said Creepy McGoo.

"She is?" asked Manager Manly. "You're sure?"

Creepy McGoo was sure. Manager Manly was pleased.

"OK, then, slide them under."

"I beg your pardon?"

"New procedure. You'll be manning the front desk every day. But any forms that need my attention will be slid under the door."

"I really get to stay?" asked Creepy McGoo. But the level of excitement in his voice made it all the creepier.

"Rejected!" said Manager Manly. "Go on back to the Room. And take the Wallflower Girl with you."

Creepy McGoo slunk away from the office and gestured to the Wallflower Girl, who gestured for him to stay away from her. Then he prowled back up the stairs. The Wallflower Girl went to the handicapped elevator.

"I don't see a limp!" Hank Edwards, the octogenarian security guard, said.

"Fuck you," said Wallflower Girl. She got on and

pushed the *Close Door* button.

Having disapproved Creepy McGoo's request to stay in the Department of Human Capital, Manager Manly quickly APPROVED the first three forms that Creepy McGoo slipped under the door: the resignation from Future Lead Underwriter Aliyah Deere, AIS, CIC, ARM, CPCU, PLCS, CLU, CRM, CV, Ms. Noreen's application for early retirement, and Monsieur Richard's request for short-term disability. He stamped Monsieur Richard's request for Worker's Compensation *INCOMPLETE*. Then he *REJECTED* Mr. Howard's resignation. He put all five documents in the *OUT* tray.

"Carol!" he called out. "Carol!"

Carol tottered in. Manager Manly pointed to his *OUT* tray. Carol collected the items, carried them to her desk and put them in her *IN* tray. She completed the required paperwork, stuffing three envelopes with congratulatory letters, one with a generic request for more information, and a final one with a blanket rejection. Then she carried them to John Doe.

"Where should I put these?"

John Doe indicated his *IN* tray, without taking his eyes off his computer screen.

Processing. Please Wait. Carol paused for a moment to view the results of the scan.

Processing. Please Wait. Processing. Upload Complete.

"Would you look at that?" said Carol when the form appeared on the screen.

CITY SCHOOLS FORM 2.1.4 B
ADMINISTRATIVE LEAVE

Administrator: _Francine Fehler_   School ID: _405_ .

Employee's Name: _Ellen Alloway_   Employee ID: _065201_ .

Reason for leave: Please select all that apply.

- ○   Gross Misconduct
- ○   Refusal to complete required duties
- ○   Endangerment to students
- ○   Allegations from third party (if selected, attach allegations separately using form 2.1.5A.)
- ○   Refusal to cooperate with administration (if selected, please describe below)

   ☑   Other (if selected, please describe below)

    Pending investigation

Employee Statement of Acknowledgement:
By signing the form, I acknowledge that I understand the reason for my leave and agree to the conditions of administrative leave as outlined in the employee agreement, which may include Room assignment, temporary re-assignment, or filing duty.

_____ Date:_____

Principal or Administrative Signature
By signing the form, I hereby release the stated employee to the authority of the City School Central Office and agree to the terms outlined in the employee agreement in conjunction with the terms decided upon by City School Central Office.

Francine Fehler _____ Date: _1/26_

For Office of Human Capital Use Only
Date of form completion:
Expected length of leave:
Reassignment Location (if applicable):

John Doe looked. And then he saw something.

"Carol," he said. "What's this box at the bottom used for?" He pointed to the *For Office of Human Capital Use Only* section.

"Oh!" said Carol. "That's where I write today's date, and then *indefinite*, and then *Re-assignment Room*. I must have missed that one."

As Carol reached for the paper, John Doe had his 'aha' moment.

"Don't worry about this one," he said. "I'll handle it."

28

Ms. Alloway stared at the basket of food that the middle-aged guy in the Yellow Kingz hat handed her. Every item was the exact same golden color. She couldn't tell the fries apart from the lake trout pieces. Ms. Alloway sighed.

She turned to the small seating area. It was empty. She was a few minutes early. She set down her basket of food and allowed her teacher bag to slide off her shoulder. She was about to put it on the floor—but then she looked at the floor. She set it up on the table with her. She picked at her food, which all tasted the same.

Creepy McGoo walked in. He smiled at her. Ms. Alloway quickly took evasive action. She removed her documentation binding and opened it up, so there was no more room at the table. Creepy McGoo frowned.

Ms. Alloway allowed herself to be absorbed in the folder's contents. She had flipped to the Jazmine Williams pages, the section she had just completed that afternoon. She had hoped that when she finished her reorganization project she would have some greater understanding about what, exactly, she had been able to achieve as a teacher. She hoped the fragments might reveal something profound. Instead, so far, it appeared to be yet another exercise in futility.

She wiped her greasy hands on her napkin and began flipping through her latest pages.

WILLIAMS, JAZMINE

| SCHOOL 405 – PHONE LOG |||||
| Teacher: *Alloway* |||||
Date	Student	Reason	Number	Result
8/29	*Jazmine W.*	*Absent the first week of school.*	██████	*Guardian: They don't go to school before Labor Day*

OFFICE REFERAL – CITY SCHOOL 401
Student: *Jazmine Williams*   **Date:** *9/3*
Referring Teacher: *Alloway*   **Location:** *201*
Description of behavior leading to referral: *Jazmine said it was hot as a whore, and I told her to watch her mouth. Jazmine then said that no bitch-ass teacher was going to tell her what to do, and I assigned detention. Then she told me what to do with my detentions. And I told her that if she wants to be a part of this class, she'll have to follow the rules. Then she belched.*

Please indicate all classroom interventions employed prior to this referral

☑ Verbal Warning ☐ Assignment Modification
☐ Written Warning ☐ Parent/Teacher Conference
☐ Seating Change ☐ Hallway "fireside" chat
☐ Positive Incentives ☐ Classroom Privilege Removal
☑ Detention ☐ Classroom Privilege Bestowal
☑ Phone Call Home ☐ Other _____

Is this a repeated issue in your classroom? *No*

Administrative Response
☐ Detention
☐ Phone call home
☐ Parent Conference
☐ Suspension
☑ Other *Student returned to class.*

Comments: *Ms Alloway, I would expect a third year teacher to be able to handle minor classroom infractions* .

Teacher Signature: *E Alloway*   **Date:** *9/3*

Principal Signature: *Francine Fehler*   **Date:** *9/3*

NAME: **Jazmine**   DATE: **9/12**

GRAMMAR EXERCISE
Their/they're/there   o⁵

Directions: Complete each sentence with *their, there,* or *they're.*

1. **Ms. Alloway** going to clean **her dirty ass** room.

2. _____ is going to be a concert tomorrow.

3. Bob and Joe said that _____ planning to go over _____ after _____ dad gets off work.

169

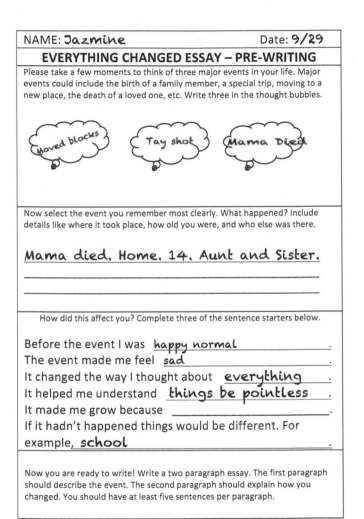

NAME: Jazmine   Date: 9/29

EVERYTHING CHANGED ESSAY – PRE-WRITING

Please take a few moments to think of three major events in your life. Major events could include the birth of a family member, a special trip, moving to a new place, the death of a loved one, etc. Write three in the thought bubbles.

Moved blocks   Tay shot   Mama Died

Now select the event you remember most clearly. What happened? Include details like where it took place, how old you were, and who else was there.

Mama died. Home. 14. Aunt and Sister.
_____
_____

How did this affect you? Complete three of the sentence starters below.

Before the event I was happy normal   .
The event made me feel sad   .
It changed the way I thought about   everything   .
It helped me understand things be pointless   .
It made me grow because _____ .
If it hadn't happened things would be different. For example, school   .

Now you are ready to write! Write a two paragraph essay. The first paragraph should describe the event. The second paragraph should explain how you changed. You should have at least five sentences per paragraph.

```
┌─────────────────────────────────────────────┐
│         FIRESIDE CHAT TRANSCRIPT              │
├─────────────────────────────────────────────┤
│ STUDENT: Jazmine Williams     DATE: 9/30     │
│ TEACHER: Alloway             LOCATION: 201   │
│                                               │
│ Alloway: You seemed like you were working     │
│ hard yesterday. Do you mind if I take a look  │
│ at what you have so far?                      │
│                                               │
│ J. Williams: You goin' to, I guess.           │
│                                               │
│ Alloway: Jazmine, this is good!               │
│                                               │
│ J. Williams: It hard.                         │
│                                               │
│ Alloway: You make it seem easy, though.       │
│                                               │
│ J. Williams: Hard means good, Ms. Alloway.    │
│                                               │
│ Alloway: Oh. Well, it's touching.             │
│                                               │
│ J Williams: Yeah?                             │
│                                               │
│ Alloway: Yeah. If you put a title on it,      │
│ I'll hang it on the good work wall.           │
│                                               │
│ J. Williams: Really?                          │
└─────────────────────────────────────────────┘
```

MAMA DIED
By Jazmine Williams

Everything changed after my mama died. Before I was happy normal I played with my sister and made up games. I made good grades in school and liked my teachers.

I remember it all clearly. My aunt called the school and said I should come home. I go home and my aunt be crying. My little sister keep asking whats wrong. Over and over. My sister six and I eight. I don't cry. I just watch them carry her out.

After it happened, I was a changed person. I no longer made up games. I just watch television and try not to think about it. Don't care about school because I know school don't really matter now. Probably my mama would be sad about how I turned out. And sometimes I want to change but how can I change when she left me.

RIP
JADA WILLIAMS
WITH THE ANGELS

GREAT
WORK!

20/20

NAME: **Jazmine**   DATE: **10/1**

GRAMMAR EXERCISE
Too/two/to   2/4

1. I went __to__ the store.

2. I bought __two__ boxes of cat litter.

3. The boxes were __to__ heavy __too__ carry.

NAME: **Jazmine Williams**
DATE: **10/2**

READING RESPONSE
"SALVATION" by Langston Hughes

I think I understand what happened to Langston. Sometimes, it feel like the whole world is crazy or frontin' or something. But you supposed to play along. But he shouldn't cry about it so much. He must be from the County.

OFFICE REFERAL – CITY SCHOOL 401

Student: *Jazmine Williams*   **Date:** *10/3*

Referring Teacher: *Alloway*   **Location:** *201*

Description of behavior leading to referral: *Jazmine wrote on the desk. I told her that she would have to wash it off. Jazmine stood up and said, "You be frontin' like you care one minute and the next minute you be snitching." Then she told me to "fuck off" and walked out of the classroom.*

Please indicate all classroom interventions employed prior to this referral

☐ Verbal Warning   ☑ Assignment Modification
☐ Written Warning   ☐ Parent/Teacher Conference
☐ Seating Change   ☐ Hallway "fireside" chat
☑ Positive Incentives   ☐ Classroom Privilege Removal
☐ Detention   ☐ Classroom Privilege Bestowal
☑ Phone Call Home   ☐ Other _____

Is this a repeated issue in your classroom? *No*

Administrative Response
☐ Detention
☐ Phone call home
☐ Parent Conference
☐ Suspension
☑ Other *Student returned to class.*

Comments: *Jazmine said that you never had a fireside chat. Please ACTUALLY intervene internally before referring a student. Thanks!*

Teacher Signature: *E Alloway*   **Date:** *10/3*

Principal Signature: *Francine Fehler*   **Date:** *10/3*

NAME: *Jazmine*   DATE: **10/8**

GRAMMAR EXERCISE
Modifiers   0 |6

Directions: Underline the modifiers in the sentences below.

1. <u>The very ugly dog barked loudly for the entire night.</u>

2. <u>On hot days, I like to swim.</u>

3. <u>My favorite book is To Kill a Mockingbird.</u>

FIRESIDE CHAT TRANSCRIPT

STUDENT: Jazmine Williams   DATE: 10/9
TEACHER: Alloway   LOCATION: 201

Alloway: First of all, *this* is a fireside chat.

J. Williams: I know what you call it.

Alloway: So why did you tell Principal Fehler that we didn't have them?

J. Williams: I didn't tell that bitch nothing.

Alloway: Watch your language.

J. Williams: What? That lady be trippin'.

Alloway: I feel like you haven't been working up to your potential recently. First quarter report cards are coming, you know.

J. Williams: You goin' fail me anyway.

Alloway: Am I the one causing you to fail? Would you want me to pass you with the effort you put in?

J. Williams: Yeah!

Alloway: Don't you think you could be doing more to help yourself out? Look at this grammar exercise.

Jazmine: I get the to/too thing now.

Alloway: But now we're on to parts of speech. You didn't even make an effort.

J. Williams: What? You didn't say NOT to underline the words that aren't modifiers.

[pause]

J. Williams: See what I mean? *You* failing me.

Alloway: Well, I'll add those points back in. But those points aren't enough, you know? You've just been spending most of class talking to Dontay and Erica.

J. Williams: Maybe if you had an interesting assignment once in awhile.

Alloway: Well, we'll be writing persuasive essays soon. I hope you will work as hard on this one as you did on the last one. It's really your only chance to get your grade up.

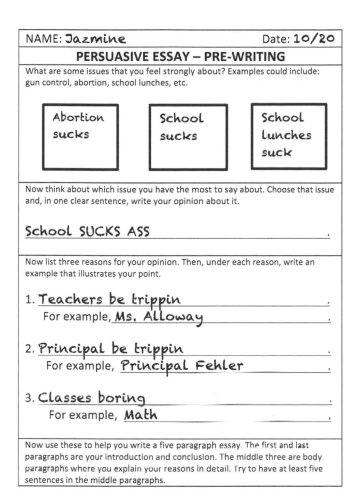

NAME: **Jazmine**   Date: **10/20**

PERSUASIVE ESSAY – PRE-WRITING

What are some issues that you feel strongly about? Examples could include: gun control, abortion, school lunches, etc.

| **Abortion sucks** | **School sucks** | **School lunches suck** |

Now think about which issue you have the most to say about. Choose that issue and, in one clear sentence, write your opinion about it.

School SUCKS ASS .

Now list three reasons for your opinion. Then, under each reason, write an example that illustrates your point.

1. **Teachers be trippin** .
   For example, **Ms. Alloway** .

2. **Principal be trippin** .
   For example, **Principal Fehler** .

3. **Classes boring** .
   For example, **Math** .

Now use these to help you write a five paragraph essay. The first and last paragraphs are your introduction and conclusion. The middle three are body paragraphs where you explain your reasons in detail. Try to have at least five sentences in the middle paragraphs.

School Sucks
By Jazmine

School sucks. Teacher be fake and don't care. Principal be crazy. And we don't learn anything useful.

CITY CHECK-UP EXAM – 1st Quarter

Student: Williams, Jazmine
Teacher: Alloway, Ellen
Subject: English

Please use blue or black ink or a number two pencil. Fill in the circle completely. No stray marks.

Right: ●

Wrong: ⊗ ☞

1	Ⓐ Ⓑ **Ⓒ** Ⓓ	11	Ⓐ Ⓑ **Ⓒ** Ⓓ
2	Ⓐ Ⓑ **Ⓒ** Ⓓ	12	Ⓐ Ⓑ **Ⓒ** Ⓓ
3	Ⓐ Ⓑ **Ⓒ** Ⓓ	13	Ⓐ Ⓑ **Ⓒ** Ⓓ
4	Ⓐ Ⓑ **Ⓒ** Ⓓ	14	Ⓐ Ⓑ **Ⓒ** Ⓓ
5	Ⓐ Ⓑ **Ⓒ** Ⓓ	15	Ⓐ Ⓑ **Ⓒ** Ⓓ
6	Ⓐ Ⓑ **Ⓒ** Ⓓ	16	Ⓐ Ⓑ **Ⓒ** Ⓓ
7	Ⓐ Ⓑ **Ⓒ** Ⓓ	17	Ⓐ Ⓑ **Ⓒ** Ⓓ
8	Ⓐ Ⓑ **Ⓒ** Ⓓ	18	Ⓐ Ⓑ **Ⓒ** Ⓓ
9	Ⓐ Ⓑ **Ⓒ** Ⓓ	19	Ⓐ Ⓑ **Ⓒ** Ⓓ
10	Ⓐ Ⓑ **Ⓒ** Ⓓ	20	Ⓐ Ⓑ **Ⓒ** Ⓓ

Williams, Jazmine Alloway, Ellen English III Simple Grade Pro Single Student Grade Summary – First Quarter			
Category	**Category Weight**	**Points Possible**	**Points Earned**
Daily assignments and homework (such as reading responses)	40%	500	201
Participation (including discussions and review games)	10%	500	184
Major essays/projects	40%	200	120
Tests (including Check-up participation)	10%	100	45
			Overall Grade: 49

SCHOOL 405
Great Kids, Great Teachers, Great Scores!

Memo

To: All teachers
From: Principal Fehler
Date: 9:00 AM 10/31
RE: First Quarter Grades

Teachers, grades are due on November 3 at 3.00. Please
keep in mind the following guidelines.

1. You must include at least one comment per student
    to clarify the reason for their grade. You may include
    up too two.
2. Students who fail must be given grades of 50 or 55.
    No other grades will be accepted.
3. You may only fail a student if you completed all steps
    below:
    a. Sent home a failing progress report
    b. Have evidence of a minimum of two fireside
        chats
    c. Called the students house regarding grades.

Remember, it is our duty to do everything we can to ensure
the success of our students. This includes high standards and
also accountability on the teachers part.

SCHOOL 405
Great Kids, Great Teachers, Great Scores!!

Memo

To: All teachers
From: Principal Fehler
Date: 10:30 AM 10/31
RE: First Quarter Grades Memo

IT IS UNNECESSARY FOR ANY MORE TEACHERS TO RETURN GRAMMATICALLY CORRECTED MEMOS. THOSE WERE TYPOS! Also, some of you asked if you have to have fireside chats with students who were chronically absent. Let me quote the district PROJECT INCREASE GRADUATION PLAN:

> 2.1.7: With regard to grades, teachers must take responsibility for the students in their classroom and the methods by which they are evaluated. Such evaluations reflect as much upon the teacher as they do on the student. If a teacher is absolutely certain that a student does not merit a passing mark, it is important for the teacher to make every effort possible to identify the underlying reason for the student's lack of success and correct it. The most proficient teachers don't make excuses for their lack of efficacy.

SCHOOL 405

Great Kids, Great Teachers, Great Scores!

First Quarter Report Card
Williams, Jazmine

Subject	Teacher	1st Quarter Grade	Total Absences	Comments
English III	Alloway	55	13	b,d
Algebra	Eagleton	60	15	d
French I	Richard	55	22	d,e
SAT Prep	Jackson	61	33	c

Comment key:
   a.   a pleasure to have in class
   b.   shows potential
   c.   shows Improvement
   d.   behavior affects classroom performance
   e.   too many absences

CITY CHECK-UP SCORES:

English - 6/20 (unsatisfactory)
Algebra - 3/20 (unsatisfactory)

Parent/Guardian Signature_____ Date:_____

FIRESIDE CHAT TRANSCRIPT

STUDENT: Jazmine Williams   DATE: 11/4
TEACHER: Alloway   LOCATION: 201

Alloway: So you are just not going to talk to me?

[Pause]

Alloway: I'm not going to end this chat until you say something.

[Pause]

[Pause]

Alloway: Seriously, we can just hang like this all day.

[Pause]

J. Williams: What good do these do? You just going to fail me. You the only teacher, too. Besides Richard!

Alloway: Did you think you deserved to pass my class?

J. Williams: I passed algebra and I only turned in two assignments. And I don't even know where my last class is. They must have moved it from the computer lab after that pipe broke.

Alloway: Well, you get a clean slate in here now. The semester grade is the important one anyway. You can easily get this one up. We're doing our poetry unit, anyway. It's a fun one.

Name: **Jazmine Williams**
Date: **11/4**

RHYME SCHEMES!

Good work.
But be nice to
Janae.
15/15

Now it's your turn! Write an original poem using the specified rhyme scheme.

RYHME SCHEME ABAB:

How many people have to die
Whys this place so shitty
I have to close my eye
Or else just leave the city

RYHME SCHEME AABB:

Janae is super fat
Why she look like that
Don't she want to be hot?
I can say she not.

RHYME SCHEME ABAB CDCD:

This school is hot
I want to eat
Dontay smokes pot
I hate this seat

I watch the clock
It moves slow
But I can't talk
Where does time go?

E.J. ROLLER

NAME: Jazmine	DATE: 11/24

Literary Devices
Practice   2/3

Directions: Write an original example of each device listed.

1. Simile - *You ugly as a toothless whore*

2. Metaphor – *You a toothless whore* .

3. Personification – *You the bigest toothless whore in the world* .

188

HEY JAZMINE!

    HEY ERICA!

I'M BORED

    ME TOO

I DON'T WANT TO GO TO FRENCH. MON. RICHARD IS A DICK.

    FOR REAL.

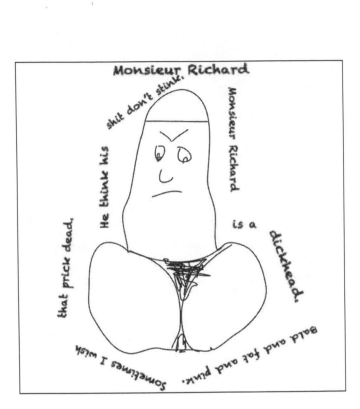

NAME: Jazmine Williams
DATE: 12/22

READING RESPONSE
"Still I Rise" by Maya Angelou

I used to think all poems were stupid, but this ones pretty good. I think Maya is trying to say that no matter what happens she can get through it. I think that's a good message but not as easy as it sounds. But I'm going to try an remember this one.

| SCHOOL 405 – PHONE LOG |||||
| Teacher: *Alloway* |||||
Date	Student	Reason	Number	Result
12/18	*Jazmine W.*	*Positive!* *Showing* *improvement.*	███████	*Guardian:* *Ok, then.*

FIRESIDE CHAT TRANSCRIPT

STUDENT: Jazmine Williams   DATE: 12/19
TEACHER: Alloway   LOCATION: 201

J. Williams: You called my house!

Alloway: Yes, but it was a good call.

J. Williams: I know. My grandma tried to scare me though.

Alloway: I bet she's proud of you.

[Pause]

Alloway: So, you have any plans for Christmas?

J. Williams: Just presents.

[Pause]

Alloway: Well, your poetry was really good this semester.

J. Williams: Fucking hard, you mean.

Alloway: Don't ruin it.

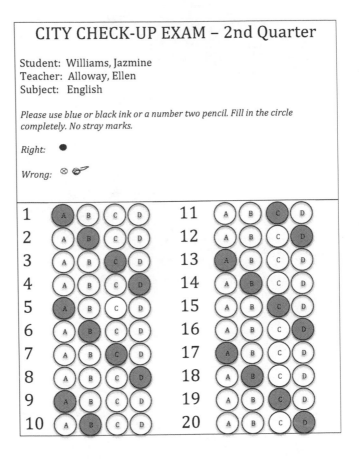

CITY CHECK-UP EXAM – 2nd Quarter

Student: Williams, Jazmine
Teacher: Alloway, Ellen
Subject: English

Please use blue or black ink or a number two pencil. Fill in the circle completely. No stray marks.

Right: ●

Wrong: ⊗ ✎

1	Ⓐ Ⓑ Ⓒ Ⓓ	11	Ⓐ Ⓑ Ⓒ Ⓓ
2	Ⓐ Ⓑ Ⓒ Ⓓ	12	Ⓐ Ⓑ Ⓒ Ⓓ
3	Ⓐ Ⓑ Ⓒ Ⓓ	13	Ⓐ Ⓑ Ⓒ Ⓓ
4	Ⓐ Ⓑ Ⓒ Ⓓ	14	Ⓐ Ⓑ Ⓒ Ⓓ
5	Ⓐ Ⓑ Ⓒ Ⓓ	15	Ⓐ Ⓑ Ⓒ Ⓓ
6	Ⓐ Ⓑ Ⓒ Ⓓ	16	Ⓐ Ⓑ Ⓒ Ⓓ
7	Ⓐ Ⓑ Ⓒ Ⓓ	17	Ⓐ Ⓑ Ⓒ Ⓓ
8	Ⓐ Ⓑ Ⓒ Ⓓ	18	Ⓐ Ⓑ Ⓒ Ⓓ
9	Ⓐ Ⓑ Ⓒ Ⓓ	19	Ⓐ Ⓑ Ⓒ Ⓓ
10	Ⓐ Ⓑ Ⓒ Ⓓ	20	Ⓐ Ⓑ Ⓒ Ⓓ

SCHOOL 405
Great Kids, Great Teachers, Great Scores!

Memo

To: All teachers
From: Principal Fehler
Date: 9:00 AM 1/9
RE: First Semester Grades

Teachers, grades are due on January 12 at 3.00. Please keep in mind the following guidelines:

1. You must include at least one comment per student to clarify the reason for their grade. You may include up too two.
2. Students who fail must be given grades of 50 or 55. No other grades will be accepted.
3. You may only fail a student if you completed all steps below:
   a. Sent home a failing progress report
   b. Have evidence of a minimum of two fireside chats
   c. Called the students house regarding grades.

ALSO, SEMESTER GRADES WILL BE CALCULATED AS FOLLOWS: 1st quarter grade = 40%; 2nd quarter grade = 40%; Semester Final = 20%. YOU MUST GIVE A FINAL. You may choose to use the **CITY CHECK-UP** or create your own, but you absolutely must give a final. As required by the district. PLEASE SEND A COPY OF YOUR FINAL TO THE OFFICE, FOR APPROVAL.

Name:_____   Date:_____

ENGLISH III FINAL

PART ONE: In the space below, write a sonnet that includes at least one simile, one metaphor, one example of hyperbole, and one example of personification.

PART TWO: On the back of this page, write a well-structured five-paragraph essay describing three things you learned this semester.

FRANCINE FEHLER <ff405@cityschools.edu> *Jan. 7*
To: Ellen Alloway <ea405@cityschools.edu>
re: Your Final

Ms. Alloway, your final concerns me. It appears subjective. You should just use the City Check-up.
Thanks!

ELLEN ALLOWAY <ea405@cityschools.edu> *Jan. 8*
To: Francine Fehler <ff405@cityschools.edu>
re: re: Your Final

Principal Fehler,
I do not believe the City Check-up is an accurate measurement of what I taught this semester. I believe the best way to assess English language skills and to promote the creative use of language is through original writing.
Thanks for your concern.

FRANCINE FEHLER <ff405@cityschools.edu> *Jan 9*
To: Ellen Alloway <ea405@cityschools.edu>
re: re: re: Your Final

Ms. Alloway, I would strongly advise you to reconsider. Objective assessments are key.

ELLEN ALLOWAY <ea405@cityschools.edu> *Jan. 9*
To: Francine Fehler <ff405@cityschools.edu>
re: re: re: re: Your Final

I attached a rubric.

English III First - Semester Final - Rubric
(Note: Finals will be handed back with further comments.)

Student: *Jazmine Williams*

Mastery of Concepts: The writing demonstrated mastery of literary devices, poetic forms, and five-paragraph structure.	9/10
Creativity: The writing was all original and demonstrated deep thinking.	5/5
Grammar: The writing included no major grammatical mistakes.	3/5
	Overall Grade: 85

Williams, Jazmine Alloway, Ellen English III Simple Grade Pro Single Student Grade Summary – Second Quarter			
Category	**Category Weight**	**Points Possible**	**Points Earned**
Daily assignments and homework (such as reading responses)	40%	500	367
Participation (including discussions and review games)	10%	500	402
Major essays/projects	40%	200	168
Tests (including Check-up participation)	10%	100	45
			Overall Grade: 76

FIRESIDE CHAT TRANSCRIPT

STUDENT: Jazmine Williams   DATE: 1/15
TEACHER: Alloway   LOCATION: 201

J. Williams: Just to warn you, I have 'foul language' in my Jim Crow law skit. Is it OK to say it in the presentations?

Alloway: You're asking permission?

J. Williams: You don't have to be smart about it.

Alloway: I'm sorry. What is the word?

J. Williams: Shit.

Alloway: Shit?

J. Williams: Shit.

Alloway: I don't think *shit* will offend anyone's delicate sensibilities.

J. Williams: What about *fuck*?

Alloway: Stick with *shit*.

Name: **Jazmine**　　　　　　　　　　　　Date: **1/16**

To Kill a Mockingbird Pre-Reading
Jim Crow Skits

Directions: Using the article we read about Jim Crow laws, please create a sketch that demonstrates the type of discrimination black people faced in that time period.

White Man: Where do you think you're going?

Black Man: I'm just taking a piss, sir.

White Man: Not there you aren't.

Black Man: But sir, it's an emergency.

White Man: You have your own spot out back.

Black Man: But they don't have any toilet paper, sir.

White Man: That's your problem. [white man goes into bathroom]

Black Man: Shit.

Name: **Jazmine**   Date: **1/16**

To Kill a Mockingbird Reading Journal
Instructions

1. Please put your name, class period, and To Kill a Mockingbird Reading Journal on the cover
2. On the first page, write Table of Contents
3. Skip two pages
4. On the next page, write "Prediction"
5. Under Prediction, make a prediction about what you think this book we'll be about, based on its cover and synopsis.

Going forward, each day you will have a prompt that relates to our reading for the day. Please use a new page for each prompt.

PREDICTION

I can't tell what this book will be about. Maybe some birds get killed. Pigeons be rats with wings.

PROMPT: Describe your family and how being a part of your family has affected you.

My family a mess. Never met my dad, but I know his name but I don't want to. My sister is a brat now and always taking my shit. Thinks she grown. My grandma ok but old and bossy. She fussing all the time and making us go to church like lanston hues. But none of it bothers me none. I'm me no matter what.

FRANCINE FEHLER <ff405@cityschools.edu> *Jan. 23*
To: Ellen Alloway <ea405@cityschools.edu>
re: re: re: re: re: Your Final

SEE ME!

"The question is, how's it going to end?" said a disembodied voice behind her left shoulder. For a terrifying moment, she thought it was Creepy McGoo. But, on turning, she saw the forgettable face of the John Doe.

He took a seat across from her and slid *Form 2.1.4* in front of her.

"I know how it *could* end," he said. "I just need you to sign this."

"Oh!" said Ms. Alloway. "I'm not falling for that! Principal Fehler set this whole thing up, didn't she?"

Ms. Alloway stood and started to crumple the form.

"Wait! Sit!" said John Doe. "Principal Fehler doesn't know I'm here."

"That's exactly what someone who *was* sent from Principal Fehler would say."

"But it's also exactly what someone who *wasn't* sent from Principal Fehler would say."

Ms. Alloway hesitated a moment. John Doe had a point. If there was one thing she'd learned from teaching in the City, it was that everyone was always saying the same thing to accomplish very different goals.

"So how do I know whose side you're really on?" asked Ms. Alloway.

"I'm not on any side," said John Doe. "I'm just trying to not make things worse," said John Doe. "First step to making the school better is to stop making it worse."

Ms. Alloway couldn't argue with that. "And what's the second step?" she asked.

John Doe shrugged.

Ms. Alloway thought that was the most honest response she'd ever received to the question.

"Just take another look at the form," he said.

"I've seen the form," she protested as she began reading it again.

After a moment or two of silence, John Doe pointed to her basket. "You gonna eat that onion ring?"

"What onion ring?" Ms. Alloway asked without taking her eyes from the form. She had made it to the bottom—and then she saw it.

"Wait a second!" Ms. Alloway said. John Doe waited. "So you're saying—"

"There's no substitute for the real thing but the real thing."

Ms. Alloway signed the form.

John Doe nodded, retrieved the onion ring from her basket, and tossed it into his mouth.

29

The next morning, Ms. Alloway drove straight to School 405 and marched to the main office, where she was promptly ignored.

"Excuse me!" she said, waving her hand in Ms. Noreen's face.

Ms. Noreen looked up from her book. She saw Ms. Alloway, rolled her eyes, and picked up her Walkie Talkie.

"Code magenta," she said. "Code magenta." Then she set the Walkie Talkie back on the desk and picked her book back up.

Principal Fehler burst out of her inner office into the outer office.

"What's the meaning of this!" she demanded. "You're supposed to be at South Avenue!"

"South Avenue sent me here," said Ms. Alloway, handing her *Form 2.1.4.* "Read the *For office use only* box."

Principal Fehler read the box aloud. "*Expected Length of Leave: Indefinite. Reassignment Location: Room 201 in School 405.*"

"What's this mean?"

"It means I've been indefinitely reassigned as a substitute for myself."

"They can't do that!"

"They *can* do that."

"They *can't* do that!"

"Why not?"

"Why *not!*"

"They did it."

"They *can't* do it!"

"I should probably get to my classroom."

"Noreen!" said Principal Fehler, "Get me the HR Department!"

"There is no HR Department," said Ms. Noreen, casually flipping a page.

"Get me someone else, then."

"Who?"

"*Who!*"

"Who?"

"Someone who can help!" Principal Fehler wrung her hands; then she stroked her chin so hard that her mole started bleeding.

"First step to getting better is to stop making it worse," said Ms. Alloway.

"What's that supposed to mean?" Principal Fehler asked.

"There's blood on your hands," said Ms. Noreen.

"What's that supposed to mean?" asked Principal Fehler.

"Hey! Hey! Hey!" said Dr. Luney, as he walked through the door. "What's going on here? Is everyone having a terrific 405 start to their day? Ms. Alloway! Welcome back."

"What's that supposed to mean?" asked Principal Fehler. "What are you all saying?"

"Ohayōgozaimasu," said Mr. White, who just popped his head in to say good morning.

Ms. Fehler crumpled to the floor.

"Is she okay?" he asked.

Ms. Noreen glanced down at Principal Fehler and shrugged.

"Looks to me like she's having a little shinkei suijaku!" Mr. White said. Then he flashed a melting smile and went on his way.

Dr. Luney drifted toward his office. "Just let me know if you need—" he said, closing the door.

"Well?" said Ms. Alloway.

Ms. Noreen shook her head and said she was counting down the days to retirement. They didn't pay her enough for this. Then she went to the closet and pulled out a pair of keys.

"Bathroom. Classroom," she said.

30

| CITY SCHOOLS FORM 2.1.4 B |
| ADMINISTRATIVE LEAVE |

Administrator: _Francine Fehler_   School ID:_405_   .

Employee's Name: _Ellen Alloway_   Employee ID:_065201_   .

Reason for leave: Please select all that apply.

- o   Gross Misconduct
- o   Refusal to complete required duties
- o   Endangerment to students
- o   Allegations from third party (if selected, attach allegations separately using form 2.1.5A.)
- o   Refusal to cooperate with administration (if selected, please describe below)

- ☒   Other (if selected, please describe below)

      Pending investigation

Employee Statement of Acknowledgement:
By signing the form, I acknowledge that I understand the reason for my leave and agree to the conditions of administrative leave as outlined in the employee agreement, which may include Room assignment, temporary re-assignment, or filing duty.

E. Alloway   Date: 4/7

Principal or Administrative Signature
By signing the form, I hereby release the stated employee to the authority of the City School Central Office and agree to the terms outlined in the employee agreement in conjunction with the terms decided upon by City School Central Office.

Francine Fehler   Date: 1/26

| For Office of Human Capital Use Only |
| Date of form completion: **4/7** |
| Expected length of leave: **Indefinite** |
| Reassignment Location (if applicable): **Room 201 in school 405.** |

209

PROMPT: How do you feel about the book so far?

We had to start the book over even though I remember it. The beginning isn't even that good. But maybe we'll move a little faster than normal since the year is practically over.

HEY!

HEY JAZMINE!

YOU HEAR 'BOUT TY?

HE A FUCKING BITCH

SUCH A EWELL

LMFAO

FIRESIDE CHAT TRANSCRIPT

STUDENT: Jazmine Williams   DATE: 4/8
TEACHER: Alloway   LOCATION: 201

Alloway: You know note passing isn't
allowed. I had to confiscate it.

J. Williams: You back for real?

Alloway: Yes.

J. Williams: OK. We goin' finish that book?

Alloway: Yes.

J. Williams: OK.

PROMPT: Did Tom Robinson's sentence surprise you?

I knew those white people goin sentence him, but it still makes me mad to think of it. I would think even white people might see that the Ewell's just trash. Almost feel sorry for how trashy they are but then they go an call Tom out his name and ruin his life.

SCHOOL 405
Great Kids, Great Teachers, Great Scores!

Memo

To: All teachers
From: Principal Fehler
Date: 9:00 AM 5/27
RE: Second Semester Grades

Teachers, grades are due on June 6 at 3.00. Please keep in mind the following guidelines:

1. You must include at least one comment per student to clarify the reason for their grade. You may include up too two.
2. Students who fail must be given grades of 50 or 55. No other grades will be accepted.
3. You may only fail a student if you completed all steps below:
    a. Sent home a failing progress report
    b. Have evidence of a minimum of two fireside chats
    c. Called the students house regarding grades.

ALSO, SEMESTER GRADES WILL BE CALCULATED AS FOLLOWS: 3rd quarter grade = 40%; 4th quarter grade = 40%; Semester Final = 20%. YOU MUST GIVE A COMPREHENSIVE FINAL. THIS IS A DISTRICT REQUIREMENT. For teachers in tested subjects: **You MUST use the CITY CHECK-UP FINAL as part of your final**, though you can add supplements. PLEASE SEND A COPY OF YOUR FINAL TO THE OFFICE, FOR APPROVAL.

Name: Jazmine Williams   Date:_____

ENGLISH III FINAL

PART ONE: Complete the City Check-Up in the manner which we discussed in class.

PART TWO: Write an essay in which you compare yourself to three different characters in *To Kill a Mockingbird*.

I'm going to compare myself to three characters: Atticus, Tom, and Scout.

I'm not much like Atticus. Not just because he a white man. Actually, he a good person. But he never gets upset about anything. I get mad all the time. I think he would be a good dad.

Tom Robinson is the black man on trial. Sometimes, I feel like I'm getting blamed for things I don't do, too. Sometimes it feels like things don't change much. But they might be a little better. We have to ask for permission to use the bathroom, but at least we all use the same ones. They dirty though.

Scout is my favorite character. Even though she white, she reminds me of me. She not shy, and she smart, and she sometimes gets into trouble. But she has a good heart. If Scout didn't sound like a boy and if Jean Louise weren't such a cracker name no offense, I would name one of my future babies that. Maybe Louise. Or Harper for the author. If my kids were like Scout, I think I'd be proud.

In conclusion, that's about it. My hand's tired. Have a nice summer.

SCHOOL 405

Great Kids, Great Teachers, Great Scores!

Fourth Quarter Report Card
Williams, Jazmine

Subject	Teacher	3rd Quarter Grade	4th Quarter Grade	Semester Final	SEMESTER GRADE	Total Absences	Comments
English III	Alloway	55	76	85	70	6	a
Algebra	Eagleton	55	65	60	60	25	d
Yearbook	Wallace	80	79	80	80	40	d,e
SAT Prep	Jackson	60	55	60	60	40	c, b

Comment key:
a. a pleasure to have in class
b. shows potential
c. shows improvement
d. behavior affects classroom performance
e. too many absences

CITY CHECK-UP SCORES:

English - 6/20 (unsatisfactory)
Algebra - 14/20 (unsatisfactory)

Parent/Guardian Signature_____ Date:_____

FRANCINE FEHLER <ff405@cityschools.edu> *July 1*
To: Ellen Alloway <ea405@cityschools.edu>
re: Your End-of-Year Test Scores

Ms. Alloway,

It appears that you have a student who took an unconventional approach to the test. I hope that she is not exemplary of the rest of your students or of the "method you discussed in class" for completing the Check-Up. I have attached a copy of her scores for your review. Understand, you will be held accountable.

Thanks!

ELLEN ALLOWAY <ea405@cityschools.edu> *July 2*
To: Francine Fehler <ff405@cityschools.edu>
re: re: Your End-of-Year Test Scores

Dear Principal Fehler,

I wish I could take the credit for it. And I fully intend to use Jazmine's work as an example for future students.

Unfortunately, though, I will be unable to personally receive the accolades for this new test-taking approach due to the following portion of the new union contract:

> If a teacher requires a substitute for more than three months of the year, neither the teacher nor the substitute shall be held responsible for standardized test scores. They must simply receive an incomplete on their evaluation, pending further results.

Thanks for your concern,
Ms. Alloway

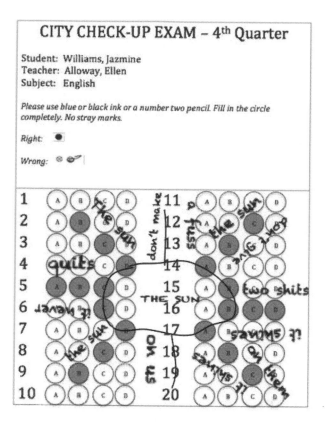

THE END.

Epilogue

Edward Winterblow staggered home from the bus stop, dropped his briefcase on the floor, and went straight for the freezer, where, lucky for him, there was a bag of frozen peas. Frozen peas, of course, are the most effective treatment for aching balls.

He limped from the freezer to the television and punched it on. Then he limped to his armchair and applied the peas bag. *Antiques Roadshow* was on, but it was a rerun. Edward Winterblow couldn't find the remote control, though, so he watched it. When his wife got home, he'd ask her to change it for him.

But, by the time his wife came home, he was engrossed in the program and had completely forgotten what it was that he was going to ask her.

"How was your day, darling?" she asked.

Edward Winterblow replied something to the effect of he was glad it was over and didn't want to talk about it, which his wife generously interpreted to mean that he was glad to be home and wanted to hear about her day. She told him what an excellent husband he was—as most men would have just wanted to talk about their day and wouldn't care a bit about

218

their wife's. Edward Winterblow had been so preoc-
cupied with trying to remember what he was going to
ask her that he'd forgotten to care about his wife's day.
But he felt certain that he would have remembered to
care if she'd just given him a little more time—and so
he accepted her praise. And when she noticed that
he'd already thawed the peas for her, which saved her
time on preparing dinner and made him the most
thoughtful husband in the world, he accepted that
praise as well.

"You know," she said, "I am a truly lucky woman."

Edward Winterblow grunted in response. He was
still trying to remember what he was going to ask his
wife.

"I was going to ask you something."

"Yes?"

"I can't remember what, though."

"Should I wait?" she asked.

Edward Winterblow considered the matter. "No,
you can go ahead and fix dinner," he said. His wife
went to the kitchen. "Oh!" Edward Winterblow called
out, "I remember now." His wife came back into the
living room. "I was going to ask you to change the
channel."

"Of course," said his wife. She moved toward the
television. "What channel would you like?"

Edward Winterblow hesitated. And a lucky hesita-
tion it was, for in that moment, the next item came up
on *Antiques Roadshow*. "Would you look at that?" asked
Edward Winterblow.

His wife, of course, looked. "It looks like an old
book."

"I have that book," said Edward Winterblow. "Get my briefcase."

His wife got his briefcase. *"Tamerlane and Other Poems.* Would you look at that?" she asked. And they both looked at it.

* * *

The night after they received the $700,000 check for *Tamerlane and Other Poems,* Edward Winterblow woke up in a sweat. He felt something, something in the pit of his stomach. Something bad. Like maybe, maybe he had done something wrong. He couldn't quite put his finger on what, exactly, was the cause of this feeling, though he had the vague impression that it had to do with that Breyona Phillips girl—or maybe the book.

He woke up his wife and explained the dilemma to her. Of course, she understood. "It's guilt, dear. But it has a cure. When I feel that way," she explained, "I go out of my way to help someone, and it goes right away."

Of course, it was good advice. And so Edward Winterblow went out of his way to his computer. He went to a website that his wife knew about called *chooseyourdonation.com.* It was a website on which City School employees could post requests and individual donors could choose which ones to fund. He figured that pledging a statistically significant portion of the check ought to do the trick.

He went to posts specific to school 405. The first one was an old one put up by one Bob Wooderson. It asked for $36.14 for a Super Sweep broom. But a mere 30-inch broom wasn't nearly enough to clear his conscience.

The next hit was posted by one Michelle Young of UCAN edUCAtioN. She was asking for $25,000 to sponsor a revolutionary test-prep concept that was guaranteed to improve student scores—and lives. That was more like it. He pledged the entire amount to the organization. And as soon as he pushed the "donate" button, he felt better. In fact, he felt down-right extravagant. With his $25,000, he single-handedly fixed the City School's test score problem.

He rewarded himself by spending an equivalent amount on a gas grill.

All that done, he crawled into his warm bed, fell asleep with a spotless conscience, and dreamt of per-fect hamburgers.

ACKNOWLEDGEMENTS

This book would not have been possible without support from Betty Gipson, William Roller, Linda Roller, and Chris Covey.

Betty Gipson provided the cover artwork and copy-edited the book; Linda Roller and Christopher Covey were the primary editors; William Roller consulted with the design of the cover and interior and took the headshot.

A big thank you, also, to Doug Roller and Jenna Roller for your encouragement.

Finally, thank you to all my former colleagues and students at Patterson, especially Mr. H. and Mr. S., who have provided consistent encouragement in my pursuits as a writer, and to my cohorts from BCTR. This book is for you all.

Did you like this book?
(A SHAMELESS PLEA FOR HELP!)

New Stein Publishing House is an independent publisher. Our marketing budget is virtually non-existent. So we are counting on readers like you to help us continue to publish high-quality books.

Here are a few things you can do to help.

    1. Think of a **friend** or two (or maybe a **teacher**) who might also appreciate the story and tell them about it. Or, better yet, just **buy the book for them**.

    2. Post about the book on **Facebook**, Twitter, Tumblr, the bathroom stall, etc. And review it on **Amazon**, Goodreads, and wherever else you shop online.

    3. If you are a person who knows people (particularly book reviewers, librarians, book store owners, bloggers etc.), please give them the information on the following page.

    4. Connect with us at **newsteinph.com** and connect with E.J. at **ejroller.com**.

For more information, feel free to contact us at information@newsteinph.com.

New Stein Publishing House

New Stein Publishing House is an independent publisher of literary short-story collections, novels, and memoirs. We take great pride in every book we publish, focusing on both content and design.

Though we rely primarily on "grassroots" marketing and online sales, we love bookstores and libraries and would love to see our books on their shelves. Our books will be available for wholesale purchase through Ingram and other major distributors approximately two months after the first release date. If you would like to see our books listed with other distributors, let us know, and we will do what we can. We can also make alternative distribution arrangements with independent booksellers.

Book reviewers: if you are interested in interviewing E.J. or reviewing *The Alloway Files*, please get in touch with us at information@newsteinph.com or with E.J. at by.jean.roller@gmail.com. We are happy to provide copies to interested reviewers.

For further information, feel free to visit our website at newsteinph.com or to contact us through email at information@newsteinph.com.

25005684R70136

Made in the USA
Charleston, SC
15 December 2013